THE COMPLETE QUANTUM LEAP BOOK

by

LOUIS CHUNOVIC

Based on the Universal Television series

QUANTUM LEAP

Created by Donald P. Bellisario

A CITADEL PRESS BOOK
Published by Carol Publishing Group

A Citadel Press Book
Published by Carol Publishing Group
Citadel Press is a registered trademark of Carol Communications, Inc.
Editorial Offices: 600 Madison Avenue, New York, N.Y. 10022
Sales and Distribution Offices: 120 Enterprise Avenue, Secaucus, N.J. 07094
In Canada: Canadian Manda Group, One Atlantic Avenue, Suite 105, Toronto,
  Ontario M6K 3E7
Queries regarding rights and permissions should be addressed to
Carol Publishing Group, 600 Madison Avenue, New York, N.Y. 10022

Carol Publishing Group books are available at special discounts for bulk purchases,
for sales promotions, fund-raising, or educational purposes. Special editions can be
created to specifications. For details contact: Special Sales Department, Carol
Publishing Group, 120 Enterprise Avenue, Secaucus, N.J. 07094

Photos courtesy of NBC.

Manufactured in the United States of America

10 9 8 7 6 5 4 3 2 1

Library of Congress Cataloging-in-Publication Data

Chunovic, Louis
    The complete Quantum leap book / by Louis Chunovic.
    —Updated ed.
        p.   cm.
    "A Citadel Press book."
    ISBN 0-8065-1699-2)pbk.)
    1. Quantum leap (Television program)   I. Title
PN1992.77.Q36C49   1995
791.45'72—dc20   95-19789
                                              CIP

For Brian and Jesse

ACKNOWLEDGMENTS

My special thanks to the creators, cast and crew of *Quantum Leap,* who, every eight or nine days during the shooting season, managed the monumental task of creating a minimovie for television.

This book is an attempt to do something special—to bring you the show's cast, crew and creators with the kind of directness and one-on-one immediacy (and with a minimum of the usual hype) that you could only get by being behind the cameras or in the stars' dressing rooms. That's because you—the *Quantum Leap* fan—are something special, too, and you've never needed hype to find the series before. Dean Stockwell puts it best:

"I've been very deeply affected by what I've felt coming back to me from the fans of this show. I've been very deeply affected by their demeanor, their sincerity, the warmth and affection that they show to the show and to Scott and myself. It's real and I think it's unique, and I've never experienced that before in my life."

Contents

INTRODUCTION

**Qué Será Será
Whatever Will Be, Will Be
The Future's Not Ours to See
Qué Será Será
What Will Be, Will Be**

Billowing white clouds boil over the horizon, clocks run frantically backward, outside a window an unearthly neon-blue light flares....

Sam Beckett, quantum physicist from the future, is leaping for the first time into another life.

He peers blearily around. In the bed next to him is a strange woman who thinks he's her husband. What's worse, she thinks it's the year 1956 and that he's a renowned test pilot, and what's worse than *that* is he knows he can't fly.

"Whoa, boy, I'm in big trouble here," he mutters, certain he must be dreaming. "Okay, it's not a dream," he thinks to himself later. "It's a nightmare, and if it's a nightmare, sooner or later there's going to be a boogieman."

What is going on? Let Albert—a boogieman if ever Sam saw one—explain it:

"I can't tell you because it's restricted. Most of what you're gonna want to know is restricted," says Al, who casually adds that he's really "a neurological hologram. It's an image only you can see and hear."

"Created by a subatomic agitation of carbon quarks tuned to the mesons of my optic neurons," Sam blurts out without thinking.

"You got it," Al replies diffidently.

"How'd I know that?" Sam wonders.

How indeed? And how does he leap from time to time and life to life? More to the point, how do *they*—the behind-the scenes creators, writers and small army of technicians—do it?

Perhaps not even Ziggy, the temperamental hybrid computer, knows. But you will. Read on...

GENESIS:
A Conversation With the
Creator of *Quantum Leap*

What Norman Lear was to *All in the Family* and Gene Roddenberry to *Star Trek,* Donald P. Bellisario is to *Quantum Leap.* He is, quite simply, the presiding genius behind the series. Without him, there would be no *Quantum Leap.*

He's also a blunt-spoken man who's been at the center of many show-business controversies. Above all, he's a writer, one of the most successful in television history.

Tell me about the genesis of *Quantum Leap.*

I have no idea about how you think of anything, I mean when you're creating a show. You sit around and thoughts come into your head.

At the time, I wanted to do a show that was different, and I wanted to do an anthological show. But that's a very dirty word to networks and studios—"anthology."

Why?

Well, because they've never really been successful, with the exception of something like, maybe, *Police Story.*

Anthological shows where you don't have a lead, every week you have a different play that you put on, just don't get an audience to tune in week after week. Everything is dependent on whatever your story is that week.

So they don't do well in syndication, and they've never been very successful. The exception to that would be Alfred Hitchcock—right?—or *The Twilight Zone,* but they were both half-hour shows and they had very strong moderators—Alfred Hitchcock and Rod Serling. So they were successful based on that.

But I wanted to do an anthology. I'd worked on a time show years ago, the concept of one. And I thought, if I do a time-travel show with a lead or a pair of leads, the audience will really like them and their relationship; and every week, as I do a different story, the audience will really be tuning in for them.

Tell me about the earlier show that you worked on.

The idea I had originally was about a guy who was living in Santa Barbara. He was a medical researcher and he found that he had a congenital disease that skipped a generation.

He knew that he would pass it on. But he knew how to stop it; they now had the drugs or the technology to know how to stop the disease from being passed on. But that didn't do him any good; he was a doomed man, unless he could go back and, in effect, inoculate his own grandfather.

Then I had him experimenting with time travel, reading everything he could and coming upon some books. That set up the travel in time. It was done by immersing yourself; you find a location that existed in the time you want to go to and you immerse yourself in the time period. And if you have enough concentration, you get there eventually. That was the rough [idea] of it.

Anyway, I was playing around with that idea the year that I created *Magnum, P.I.* so that goes back to 1979.

Did that show have a name?

I think I had a name for it, but I don't remember it. But that was back in 1979. Then I created *Magnum* and just forgot about it, and I went on from there and did a lot of other shows.

The other thing that was happening then, I was reading a book, which was nonfiction, and it discussed man's dealing with the cosmos from the beginning of time—his perception of the world, the environment, the whole universe.

So I was reading that and Einstein's theory of relativity—time and space, the fourth dimension. I was just reading that, trying to understand it. So running around in my mind there was a soup of that book and wanting to do an anthology and the time-travel thing from 1979, and out pops *Quantum Leap.*

Did it pop into your head whole?

Yeah, it just popped into my head absolutely whole. It popped into my head one morning.

I was asleep and I woke up about three in the morning, four in the morning, and it all jelled in my head.

What did you do then?

The way I normally work is I sit down and I write. I don't work it all out [first], I just sit down and write.

The first thing I wrote was an opening scene, where it was the middle of Monument Valley—this is a scene, by the way, that I've never used.

It was the middle of Monument Valley and you didn't know if it was primordial times or today, because Monument Valley, if you're in the middle of it and you're all alone, believe me, it could be a hundred-thousand years ago.

There was a cry of a bird circling high in the sky, and we came down and there was a man, and the man rolled over and he was practically naked.

He was lying there, and the man's voice started in voice-over. What you learned was that he had absolutely no idea of where he was, who he was, how he got there, couldn't remember anything of his past. It was as if he was just dropped, just born, a blank tape, into the middle of the desert. That was the start of it.

Then a sheriff stopped, picked him up, said, "Get in, Chief."

Before he got in, he needed water, he was desperately parched. He went to get the water that was hanging in an old water bag over the radiator, and he [noticed] that the license plate was 1955 or something.

He just thought, "Whoa, really out there!"

He got into the jeep and found there was a body in the back, and he was the one accused of committing the murder. Then he looked into the mirror and he was an Indian.

That's what I wrote. I wrote about a five-page scene. That got it started.

That was Sam right there being born. That was Sam.

Tell me some of the other people that were up for the two roles.

Oh God, I don't want it to get into that.

They were all basically unknowns for Sam; there were a lot of known actors for the role that Dean got, a couple of English actors. But I don't want to say it was this guy and I rejected him.

So how did you sell this to the network?

They wanted me to do a series over at NBC, so I got into a meeting with Brandon Tartikoff, Warren Littlefield, and Perry Simon [the then three senior NBC programming executives].

We sat down and they pitched me a couple of series concepts that they were interested in pursuing.

Remember what they were?

One of them was called *The Silver Surfer.* It was about an aging surfer—"aging" being someone who was in his early thirties, heh-heh—who still hit the boards.

He was the chauffeur/bodyguard/confidant of an attractive mid-forties woman, who was mayor of this small town. Everyone thought they had something going between them, but what he was, in effect, was her investigator into crimes and into problems.

The other one was about this team of misfits—kind of *The A-Team* meets *The Untouchables*—a group of misfit law-enforcement officers with various talents, who get together in Chicago or someplace to clean up the town.

They all drive really fast automobiles, have helicopters, jets, dress in Armani suits—why not?

So they pitched me these arenas, and said, "How about that?" And I said, "Let me pitch you an arena."

So I pitched them the story. The only thing I didn't have at that time, and I think I got it at the meeting, was, I said, "I don't want to travel back too far in time, because I want to have some sense of reality to the show."

I meant that. If you don't travel back too far, you get into the stories and you understand them, you totally go with them. If you go back too far, there's an unreal element to it.

If Sam suddenly leaps in with the Roman legions, or he's on an old ship sailing around the Horn, it just becomes very unrealistic. You leap him back to 1965 and put him in a '57 Chevy with a bunch of other guys and drive him up to a

drive-in burger place and throw on some rock and roll, you kind of go, "Yeah, that could be."

I had all that at the meeting, and they said, "Whoa! What controls all that?"

And then it just hit me: He can't leap beyond his own lifetime.

That just came out: He can't leap beyond his own lifetime. Sometimes you get things you want to do creatively and you don't have a reason for them. It's what I call PCR.

Meaning?

Post-Creative Rationalization. Heh-heh. It really is. "Why does it happen? Why?" Uhhhhhhhh, because, because—he can only leap within his own lifetime!

And then, out of that came my string theory about how it all works.

So it was all stuff I knew I wanted to do. When you create something, and people ask you how it works, to justify it, you go back and figure it all out. And you PCR.

So naturally Brandon and Warren, being the programming geniuses they are, saw the potential in this?

They looked at me a little askance for a while. They really went with me because they knew me and they knew my work. Both Brandon and Warren have said to me at different times, "You know, anybody else would have come in with this, we'd have probably just said, 'Bye.' But we decided to roll with you on it." They gave me an order for thirteen [episodes], then I went away to cast it.

When Scott came in, I knew he was Sam. Same with Dean.

What's the toughest show you've done?

Quantum Leap.

They've all been difficult for different reasons. *Airwolf* had aircraft and acrobatics. *Magnum* was in Hawaii.

This show's a pleasure to produce, but because of the economics...it's been very, very difficult.

By the way, my original thought on the show was that maybe I would do two, three leaps in an hour. Then they could be segmented off later [in syndication] and mixed and matched.

What are the stories you've wanted to do that you haven't done so far?

There's nothing really important we haven't done. We've talked about doing a fireman show....I've wanted to leap him into *Magnum*. We haven't done that yet.

I think I've caught you in one error.

What's that?

Ziggy. Ziggy was referred to as a male, until the "Leap Back" when Ziggy has a female voice.

Yeah, Ziggy was referred to as a male through every show. Heh, heh, heh. Yeah. But Ziggy turns out to be a she.

It's not an error. We just decided to make Ziggy a female.

I mean, it wasn't like, "Oh God, we didn't think of that!" We thought of that first thing, right off the bat, and said, "Oh, who cares?"

If you want me to PCR that one, I'll tell you that Sam didn't remember that Ziggy was a female until he came back, and Al, not wanting to spoil anything for him or throw more of a load onto him than he already had, just rode along with it. How's that?

I know an exit line when I hear one.

I just wanted to say that the show was originally put on Friday and we didn't want it there, so we got it moved to Wednesdays.

The fans found it. They tried to move it back to Fridays. We got lost there again. We came back [to Wednesdays].

That first year, the second year, what kept us on—and it was critical—was the fans. They kept us on the air, and now we're going for year five.

BACKSTORY: A
Sam Beckett Biography

Sam Beckett, the genius behind the top-secret Quantum Leap Project, is probably the only human being on earth who could figure out a way to stop himself from yo-yoing through time...if only he could remember.

Unfortunately, the out-of-control time-travel experiment has had an unexpected side effect: Sam's brain has been "magnafluxed"—or, as Al puts it, "Swiss-cheesed"—and now Sam has some difficulty remembering crucial parts of his own history or information about the future. But it's all there in Ziggy's hybrid electronic brain. A printout follows:

BECKETT, SAM

Born	1953
Birthplace:	Elk Ridge, Indiana
Parents' Names:	Mother, Thelma; Father, John (died 1974)
Parents' Occupations:	Dairy Farmers
Siblings:	Sister, Kate; Brother, Tom (service record CLASSIFIED)
Education	• Mathematics, chess and piano prodigy
	• Elk Ridge High School (varsity basketball)
	• IQ: 267
	• MIT graduate (2 years), *summa cum laude;* co-developer: "String Theory" of universal structure (see: Professor Sebastian LoNigro)
	• Holder of six doctorates, including quantum physics, medicine, ancient languages
	• Fluent in seven modern languages, including Japanese, Spanish, German, French
Other Skills:	• Reads Egyptian hieroglyphics
	• Fluent in four "dead" languages, including Latin
	• *Sensei* (master) in the martial arts of *sabbatt, mu tai, karate, judo/jujitsu*
Marital Status:	Married; was engaged to Donna Eleese, formerly of the Star Bright Project (predecessor to Quantum Leap). Marriage plans canceled by her. Currently believes that he is single (see: psychological profile created by Dr. Verbina Beeks/ACCESS RESTRICTED)
PsychoDiagnostic:	Chronic acrophobia (fear of heights)
Honors:	Winner, Nobel Prize, quantum physics

BACKSTORY: An Albert Calavicci Biography

Albert "Al" Calavicci has had a tough life. You can see it in his eyes and the line of his mouth, hear it in his sardonic tone of voice. Even his name—*calavicci* is Italian for "screwdriver"—fits the man, and the man, however much at times he might exasperate Sam, fits the job.

And what a specialized job it is. Al is The Observer, a neurological hologram. You could call him the ghost in the machine, or, perhaps, Sam Beckett's guardian angel.

He's the human link between Ziggy the parallel hybrid computer and Sam the Timer Traveler ricocheting through the past. A printout of his biography follows:

CALAVICCI, ALBERT (ADMIRAL, USN):

Born:	Date Unknown; Estimate 1940
Birthplace:	Unknown; Estimate New York (see: Manhattan Orphanage Records)
Parents' Names:	Mother, Unknown; Father, Unknown (see: FBI Central Net for aliases)
Parents' Occupations:	Mother, Unknown; Father, worked construction projects in Middle East
Siblings:	Sister, Trudy (deceased)
Education:	• Primary and secondary schooling at orphanage • Practical education: acting in little theater groups • MIT graduate • Annapolis graduate (1956)
Other Skills:	• Golden Gloves boxer • Fluent in Italian • Pilot (U.S. Navy) • Astronaut (NASA)
Service Record:	• Naval pilot, aircraft carrier (late 1950s) • Vietnam, two tours (mid-1960s) • MIA/POW, Cham Hoi Prison (1967–1973) • NASA Space Program (mid–1970s to mid–1980s) • Chief, Star Bright Program (mid-1980s to 1990) • Co-creator, Quantum Leap (1990–1999) • Current rank: Admiral, two stars
Marital Status:	• Married, five times • Divorced by his first wife while he was an MIA • Current girlfriend: Tina
PsychoDiagnostic:	Recovered alcoholic

QUANTUM LEAP: The Theory of the Future and the Theory of the Show

Leaping in at the beginning of "Future Boy," Dr. Sam Beckett, wayward time traveler, finds himself in a hokey "time machine," wearing an equally bizarre masked costume and being addressed as "Future Boy" by a crazed and over-the-hill "Captain Galaxy."

Yes, Sam has leaped in as Captain's Galaxy's sidekick in a wacky '50s kids television show called *Time Patrol*, with an avid following of *Time Cadets*.

The Captain, who's about to be committed to a mental institution by his estranged daughter, turns out to be an aging actor and a not-so-crazy inventor who's come up with the same theory that, years in the future, Sam will formulate, the very theory underpinning the Quantum Leap Project.

In Captain Galaxy's basement is a faintly Jules Vernesque homemade time machine. As Captain Galaxy—actually a batty, but endearing old actor named Moe Stein—scurries manically around in a white lab coat, he explains his growing fascination with time.

M O E

I began to read everything I could about it— Heisenberg's Theory of Indeterminacy, Planck's Hypothesis of Discrete Units, Einstein's Theory of Relativity....

S A M

Yeah, but when you say time travel...you mean like on your show?

M O E

No, no, that's fantasy. This is real!

Moe finds a piece of string and holds it up.

M O E

Time is like a piece of string...

Al, standing in the background, is starting to look amazed.

17

MOE

One end of the string is birth, the other is death. If you put them together, then your life is a loop.

Al, so astounded that he stops in mid-puff, points his cigar in Captain Galaxy's direction.

AL

Hey! Sam, that's your theory!

MOE

(still holding the looped string)

If I can travel fast enough along the loop, I will eventually end up back at the beginning of my life.

AL

He—he's got it!

SAM

(taking the string in his palm)

Well, let me ask you what would happen if you would ball the string—right?—and then each day of your life would touch another day. And then, you could travel from one place on the string to another, thus enabling you to move back and forth within your own lifetime. Maybe.

MOE

(excited)

That's it! That's it! Then I could actually...

SAM

Quantum Leap.

MOE

I like that. I like that a lot.

The "Future Boy" plot is, of course, a witty send-up of the show's own original premise. (Next time you see it, notice what a good time Dean Stockwell is having "reacting" to everything going on around Sam, who not only has to declaim his lines while wearing a costume that, as he says, makes him look like a TV dinner, but also has to do a singing commercial dressed as "Mister Scrub-O," a giant steel-wool pad.)

At the same time, "Future Boy" is an excellent example of the elements that make a *Quantum Leap* episode not only tick but resonate.

Those elements have been written down in a Story Guideline issued to prospective writers. Here—from the guideline's suggested checklist—is exactly what they're looking for:

• Is it dramatic? Currently, we're most interested in serious, really dramatic stories with heart....

The best stories seem to be in arenas that put Sam in challenging situations....

We're also interested in stories that touch the heroic dreamer in all of us, ones that put Sam in situations that we ourselves would love to be in....

Remember, though, that no matter how interesting the arena [that is, the general locale or milieu], all our stories have to have heart... an emotional core that is warm and real and that will genuinely involve us and move us.

• What is the good that Sam will do? How will he help the situation he has leaped into?

The best stories, and the ones that we prefer, have Sam as the person with the problem that must be solved....

In some stories, Sam is not the one with the problem. In these cases, he helps someone at a pivotal point in their life or when they are about to make a fork-in-the-road decision, which Sam influences and makes us feel "good" that things worked out in this new way.

Sometimes the "main" problem that Sam solves is not what causes him to leap out. Instead, it is a minor, or completely unexpected problem. This is often a humorous "Kiss With History"....

• Have you used the era? For fun and plot, make sure you can juxtapose contemporary information and/or attitudes we know today—in contrast with earlier times and places....

• What's the urgency to Sam? Is there a ticking clock? What's the urgency of the story? That is, why should we care and keep watching?.... Who is the antagonist in your story? He should be strong and believable.

• The Observer (Al)—what problems and opportunities does Al offer the story idea?...

A) Al the Observer is tricky; find the right balance of "heart"/helpfulness.... Careerwise, Al was once a fallen angel, but he is Sam's guardian angel....

B) Sometimes it is fun to give Al some minor amusing problem/subplot that is always off-camera and minuscule compared to Sam's urgent cliff-hanger....

C) Al is a "techno-ghost," a hologram who is NOT there physically—so not only is Al never seen or touched by anyone, Al CANNOT touch or affect the time and place Sam is in.

In "Future Boy," as well as most of the episodes, you can actually check off these guidelines, point by point.

What's the arena?

In "Future Boy," it's a 1957 television show for kids.

Does the plot touch the "heroic dreamer in all of us"?

In "Future Boy," at Moe's sanity hearing, Sam delivers a heartfelt speech about how dreamers must be given a chance to realize their dreams, no matter how improbable they seem.

What's the good Sam will do? What's the "ticking clock" or jeopardy?

Sam is trying to reconcile Moe with his estranged daughter, who's trying to have him committed; he knows from Al and the handlink to Ziggy, the temperamental hybrid electronic computer, that history shows Moe was killed after running away from the sanity hearing.

What's Al's subplot concern?

In "Future Boy" Al must attend a court hearing, too, called by one of his ex-wives. When Sam later asks how it went, Al drolly replies, "We decided to examine each other's briefs and call it even."

Have you used the era, juxtaposing contemporary information with earlier times?

Dressed in his "Future Boy" gear at a public appearance crowded with Time Cadets, Sam blithely explains that the future holds such items as microwave ovens and cable television.

What's the kiss with history?

"Future Boy" has an ironic "kiss." Once the main problem (reconciling Moe and his daughter) has been solved, "Captain Galaxy" makes his farewell appearance on the television show and reads a final viewer letter on the air.

That letter is from avid watcher "little Sam Beckett in Elk Ridge, Indiana," who asks, "Could you explain your theory of time travel to us?"

Captain Galaxy replies that "our lifetimes are like a piece of string, but if you roll the string up into a ball, all the days of your life..."

Instantly, Sam leaps into his next life.

Now, if you're thinking of writing a script yourself, remember:

You need a reputable agent, preferably one who knows the business and specializes in representing episodic television series writers. Like most series, *Quantum Leap* only accepts submissions through recognized agents. It's done for legal protection. You can get a list of agents who'll read your unsolicited script by contacting the Writers Guild West in Beverly Hills. The *Quantum Leap* office will never read unsolicited and unrepresented *Quantum Leap* scripts.

Remember: Almost every episode conforms to a particular structure, dictated by the main commercial, or "act,"

breaks. Here's *Quantum Leap's*, as explained by the guideline:

> Structure: A dramatic/jolting arrival moment for the Teaser [i.e., the first brief scene before the commercial break that precedes the first act], then by the end of Act One, Sam is usually told by Al what his plot goal is: what he has to do or who he has to help. Act Two is the big obstacle/complication to that, but at the end of Act Three, there's a monkey wrench thrown in the works—he learns something is fundamentally wrong or doomed about how he's proceeding—then in Act Four, he creatively finds a NEW solution to the original problem, only to usually discover that there's something else that was the correct problem to solve all along. He does and—pop—he's gone.

It sounds simple, but of course it isn't, and even the show's writers concede that they can't always harmoniously blend each element into each story.

Sometimes, an episode won't even have all of the Big Three: Heart, Humor and History. Keep the guidelines in mind as you consider the following heart/history checklist for individual episodes in the first three seasons, beginning with the 1989 pilot. All the leaps in chronological order also are included later in this volume.

Keep in mind, too, that the writers and producers were working to weave these same elements into every leap, right up to the final season's final episode. In considering the complete chronology of leaps, you can just as readily pick out these elements yourself, especially the "heart story" and the "kiss with history," in the storylines of episodes that first aired late in the show's original network run.

1989 WINTER/SPRING SEASON

Genesis

LEAP: Sam leaps in as an X-2 test pilot and a minor league baseball player.

HEART STORY: Sam saves the baby and wife of the test pilot. As the baseball player, he's there to win the game for the team.

KISS WITH HISTORY: X-2 plane testing and breaking Mach-3. Sam nicknames a military memory questionnaire "Trivial Pursuit." As the baseball player, Sam is pitched to by a young Tom Seaver.

"Double Identity," November 8, 1965

LEAP: Sam leaps in as a mob hit man.

HEART STORY: Sam helps a beautician gain her self-confidence and gets a hit man to take on a new profession.

KISS WITH HISTORY: Sam causes the 1965 Blackout that takes place in the Northeast.

"The Right Hand of God," October 24, 1974

LEAP: Sam leaps in as a has-been boxer.

HEART STORY: Sam has to win a boxing match so the nuns who own his contract can use the prize money to build a chapel for the poor.

KISS WITH HISTORY: Muhammad Ali and George Foreman fight in Zaire. Streakers seen on television racing across a football field.

"Star-Crossed," June 15, 1972

LEAP: Sam leaps in as an alcoholic English literature professor.

HEART STORY: Sam meets his ex-fiancée and reconciles her with her father and with his own feelings for her.

KISS WITH HISTORY: Sam watches the pullout from Vietnam on television. Donna's father lives in the Watergate Hotel. Sam arrives with Donna to visit him and accidentally causes the infamous break-in to be discovered.

"How the Tess Was Won," August 5, 1956

LEAP: Sam leaps in as a veterinarian for a Texas ranch.

HEART STORY: Sam helps a young woman realize she must follow her heart and find the right man.

KISS WITH HISTORY: A young boy (a.k.a. Buddy Holly), who tends the vet's animals, spends his spare time picking out tunes on his guitar. With Sam's help he writes the lyrics for "Peggy Sue."

"Play It Again, Seymour," April 14, 1953

LEAP: Sam leaps in as a hard-boiled detective à la Humphrey Bogart.

HEART STORY: Sam helps Seymour, a newspaper boy, stop living a fantasy detective life and discover his ability to write detective novels.

KISS WITH HISTORY: Sam encounters the young Woody Allen at the airport.

"Color of Truth," August 8, 1955

LEAP: Sam leaps in as a poor Southern black man who is a chauffeur for an elderly, rich white woman.

HEART STORY: Sam tries to enlighten the rich woman and the whole town.

KISS WITH HISTORY: No one moment. Civil Rights movement.

"Camikazi Kid" June 6, 1961

LEAP: Sam leaps in as a Valley hot-rodder.

HEART STORY: Sam saves the sister of a hot-rodder from an abusive marriage and supports her decision to join the Peace Corps.

KISS WITH HISTORY: Sam meets a young Michael Jackson and shows him how to moonwalk.

1989—90 SEASON

"Disco Inferno," April 1, 1976

LEAP: Sam leaps in as a movie stuntman.

HEART STORY: Sam helps the younger brother of the man he has leaped into to not be coerced by their stuntman father into becoming a stuntman. Instead, he encourages the brother to pursue his talent as a musician.

KISS WITH HISTORY: Sam uses President Gerald Ford's fall down the stairs of an airplane to win a bet and the father's support for his son.

"Blind Faith" February 12, 1964

LEAP: Sam leaps in as a blind concert pianist.

HEART STORY: Sam helps a young girl find her self-confidence and separate from her domineering mother.

KISS WITH HISTORY: Beatles Concert.

"The Americanization of Machiko," August 4, 1953

LEAP: Sam leaps in as a sailor returning home from overseas duty with a Japanese wife.

HEART STORY: Sam gets the mother of the sailor to accept his Japanese wife as an equal.

KISS WITH HISTORY: None.

"Jimmy," October 24, 1964

LEAP: Sam leaps in as Jimmy, the retarded younger brother of a married man.

HEART STORY: Sam helps Jimmy's sister-in-law to accept him and prove to coworkers his value as a competent member of society.

KISS WITH HISTORY: None.

"Good Morning, Peoria," September 9, 1959

LEAP: Sam leaps in as a disc jockey.

HEART STORY: In a battle for free speech, Sam helps a woman keeps her rock and roll radio station open against the town's pressure for censorship.

KISS WITH HISTORY: Sam teaches Chubby Checker "The Twist."

"Thou Shalt Not," February 2, 1974

LEAP: Sam leaps in as a rabbi.

HEART STORY: Sam helps a family come to terms with the accidental death of a son and keeps them from splitting up.

KISS WITH HISTORY: Sam introduces Dr. Heimlich to the Heimlich maneuver when the doctor is accidentally choking on food.

"So Help Me God," July 29, 1957

LEAP: Sam leaps in as a southern white lawyer defending a black woman accused of murdering a white man.

HEART STORY: Sam restores a black woman's hope and teaches her that if she learns to read she doesn't have to rely on others.

KISS WITH HISTORY: None.

"Honeymoon Express" April 27, 1960

LEAP: Sam leaps in as an NYPD lieutenant on his honeymoon on a train bound for Niagara Falls.

HEART STORY: Sam saves a women from her obsessive ex-husband and encourages her to pursue a career in law. Thirty-five years later, she is on the committee to decide if Sam's project merits funding.

KISS WITH HISTORY: None.

"MIA," April 1, 1969

LEAP: Sam leaps in as a rookie undercover detective in San Diego.

HEART STORY: Sam's mission is to prevent a young woman from remarrying while her husband is missing in action and presumed dead. Sam later discovers that the MIA was Al himself, the young woman Al's first wife and true love. His real mission is to prevent a fellow detective from being murdered by hippie drug pushers.

KISS WITH HISTORY: None.

"Catch a Falling Star," March 21, 1979

LEAP: Sam leaps in as an understudy in a road company of *Man of La Mancha*.

HEART STORY: Sam has to come to terms with the love he had for his piano teacher when he was fifteen and prevent an aging actor from ruining his career.

KISS WITH HISTORY: None.

"What Price Gloria?" October 16, 1961

LEAP: Sam leaps in as a blonde bombshell secretary.
HEART STORY: Sam has to convince his "roommate" to pursue her own dreams and get ahead without being dependent on a man.
KISS WITH HISTORY: None.

"A Portrait of Troian," February 7, 1971

LEAP: Sam leaps in as a parapsychologist.
HEART STORY: Sam convinces a young widow that she is not insane, hearing the voice of her drowned husband, and that allows her to go on with her life.
KISS WITH HISTORY: California's Sylmar quake.

"Another Mother," September 30, 1981

LEAP: Sam leaps in as a divorced mother of three kids.
HEART STORY: Sam helps a fifteen-year-old learn the right attitude about sex and not succumb to peer pressure.
KISS WITH HISTORY: None.

"Her Charm," September 26, 1973

LEAP: Sam leaps in as a crooked FBI agent.
HEART STORY: Sam saves a woman in the Federal Witness Protection Program from her ex-boss against whom she once testified.
KISS WITH HISTORY: None.

"Animal Frat" October 19, 1967

LEAP: Sam leaps in as a fraternity brother à la John Belushi in *Animal House.*
HEART STORY: Sam shows a woman that her antiwar goals are valid, but her methods (bombing the chemistry lab) are wrong.
KISS WITH HISTORY: None.

"All-Americans," November 6, 1962

LEAP: Sam leaps in as a Mexican-American high school quarterback in the San Fernando Valley.
HEART STORY: Sam helps a Mexican-American teammate to not forfeit his promising future in football by throwing a high school city championship.
KISS WITH HISTORY: None.

"Leaping in Without a Net," November 18, 1958

LEAP: Sam leaps in as an aerialist in a family trapeze act.
HEART STORY: Sam reconciles a father and son and restores a family trapeze act to greatness by helping the daughter perform the death-defying triple.
KISS WITH HISTORY: None.

"Pool Hall Blues," September 4, 1954

LEAP: Sam leaps in as Charlie "Black Magic" Waters, a black pool hustler.
HEART STORY: Sam helps a woman keep her blues club and her honor by winning a high-stakes game of pool.
KISS WITH HISTORY: None.

"Freedom," November 22, 1970

LEAP:	Sam leaps in as a Shoshone Indian.
HEART STORY:	Sam helps an Indian man escape from jail and life in a nursing home and return to the land of his birth to die with dignity.
KISS WITH HISTORY:	None.

"Good Night, Dear Heart," November 9, 1957

LEAP:	Sam leaps in as a mortician in Massachusetts.
HEART STORY:	Sam becomes obsessed with solving the murder of a beautiful young German woman who was presumed to have committed suicide.
KISS WITH HISTORY:	None.

"Maybe Baby," March 11, 1963

LEAP:	Sam leaps in as a bouncer-turned-kidnapper in Waco, Texas.
HEART STORY:	Sam helps a stripper reunite a baby with its real mother.
KISS WITH HISTORY:	None.

"Sea Bride," June 3, 1954

LEAP:	Sam leaps in on an ocean liner as a handsome playboy determined to win back his ex-wife on the eve of her wedding to a new husband.
HEART STORY:	Sam helps a woman avoid a marriage of convenience to a disreputable man and reunites her with her true love, her ex-husband.
KISS WITH HISTORY:	None.

1990—91 Season

"The Leap Home, Part I," November 25, 1969

LEAP: Sam leaps in as himself as a sixteen-year-old playing in a championship high school basketball game.

HEART STORY: Sam tries to get his father to give up his unhealthy habits and keep his brother from going to Vietnam, where he knows he'll get killed.

KISS WITH HISTORY: None.

"Vietnam, the Leap Home, Part II," April 7, 1970

LEAP: Sam leaps into Signalman Second Class Herbert "Magic" Williams, a Navy SEAL, in Vietnam.

HEART STORY: Sam is in his brother's squad in Vietnam, the day before Tom is killed on a POW rescue mission. Sam is there to see that the operation his brother died in is successful, and he struggles to save his life.

KISS WITH HISTORY: None.

"Black on White on Fire," August 11, 1965

LEAP: Sam leaps into Ray Jordan, a black medical student engaged to a white girl during the Watts Riot.

HEART STORY: Sam has to prevent Susan Bond from being killed during the riot. In the process, he attempts to fight bigotry on both sides.

KISS WITH HISTORY: The Watts Riot of 1965.

"Glitter Rock," April 12, 1974

LEAP: Sam leaps in as the lead singer in a glitter rock bank ...à la KISS. He must discover who murdered the band's lead singer in 1974.

HEART STORY: Sam discovers that one of the suspects, a fan who has been stalking the band, claims to be Sam's son. Sam must determine if this is true.

KISS WITH HISTORY: None.

"Runaway," July 4, 1964

LEAP: Sam leaps in as thirteen-year-old Butchie Rickett, on vacation with his family driving cross-country from Florida. Sam believes he is there to help prevent Butchie's mother from deserting the family the following day.

HEART STORY: Sam has two missions: First, he finds that Butchie's mother died in a hiking accident and he must save her from disaster. Second, Sam must reconcile his father with his mother's aspirations to finish college.

KISS WITH HISTORY: None.

"Miss Deep South," June 7, 1958

LEAP: Sam leaps in as Darlene Monty, a beauty pageant contestant.

HEART STORY: Sam's job is to help save Connie, a fellow contestant, from being blackmailed by the pageant photographer who has compromising photos of her.

KISS WITH HISTORY: None.

"Rebel Without a Clue," September 1, 1958

LEAP: Sam leaps into The Cobras, a motorcycle gang, where he is known as the "gang clown."

HEART STORY: Sam has to prevent Becky, the gang leader's girlfriend, from being murdered by her abusive old man. Sam must also persuade Becky to pursue her dream as a writer so she may become a successful novelist.

KISS WITH HISTORY: Sam meets Jack Kerouac

"Leap of Faith," August 19, 1963

LEAP: Sam leaps into Francis Giuseppe Pistano, a priest at St. Dorothy's, to help avert his own murder.

HEART STORY: Sam must restore the faith of a fellow priest.

KISS WITH HISTORY: None.

"One Strobe Over the Line," June 15, 1965

LEAP: Sam leaps in as Karl Granson, a fashion photographer.

HEART STORY: Sam has to help model Edie Landsdale prevent her own death from an overdose of pills and alcohol.

KISS WITH HISTORY: None.

"The Boogieman," October 31, 1964

LEAP: Sam leaps in as a second-rate horror novelist, Joshua Rey, on Halloween.

HEART STORY: Sam battles the Devil, in the likeness of Al. Sam also has to prevent Mary Greeley, Rey's girlfriend and research assistant, from being murdered by the Devil.

KISS WITH HISTORY: Sam meets young Stephen King and unknowingly gives him ideas for *Christine, Cujo,* and *Carrie.*

"The Great Spontini," May 9, 1974

LEAP: Sam leaps in as Harry Spontini, an amateur nightclub magician, and finds himself in the middle of a custody battle for his twelve-year-old daughter.

HEART STORY: Same must save the life of his daughter from a magic trick gone awry, reconcile with his ex-wife and reunite the family.

KISS WITH HISTORY: None.

"A Little Miracle," December 24, 1962

LEAP: Sam leaps in as Reginald Pearson, the valet to real estate tycoon Michael Blake.

HEART STORY: Sam must install the spirit of Christmas in Blake and save a mission from being torn down. He gets help from Al, who pretends to be the Ghost of Christmas Future.

KISS WITH HISTORY: None.

"Private Dancer," October 6, 1979

LEAP: Sam leaps in as Rod "The Bod" McCarty, a male stripper.

HEART STORY: Sam befriends a deaf waitress, helps to convince her that her dancing ability is worth an audition with a top dance instructor and leads her away from a life on "the streets."

KISS WITH HISTORY: None.

"Future Boy," October 6, 1957

LEAP: Sam leaps in as Future Boy, the sidekick to Captain Galaxy, a kiddie television show host.

HEART STORY: Sam has to convince Captain Galaxy's daughter not to commit her father to a mental hospital. She believes he is crazy because he is trying to build a real time machine.

KISS WITH HISTORY: Sam gives his four-year-old self the idea for Quantum Leaping.

"Piano Man," November 10, 1985

LEAP: Sam leaps in as lounge singer Chuck Tanner (a.k.a. Joey DeNardo) who has an act with Lorraine, klutz extraordinaire.

HEART STORY: Sam has to prevent himself and Lorraine from being killed, then reunite his character with Lorraine in a successful lounge act.

KISS WITH HISTORY: None.

AKA:
8½ MONTHS

"Billy Jean," November 15, 1955

LEAP: Sam leaps in as Billie Jean Crockett, a sixteen-year-old unwed mother-to-be due to give birth within thirty-six hours.

HEART STORY: Sam helps Billie Jean reconcile with her own father, and ensures that the baby will have a good life being raised by a single parent.

KISS WITH HISTORY: None.

"Southern Comforts," August 4, 1961

LEAP: Sam leaps in as the owner of a brothel in Louisiana, and finds himself pursued by the madame.

HEART STORY: Sam has to help save the madame's pregnant cousin from her abusive husband.

KISS WITH HISTORY: None.

"Last Dance Before an Execution," May 12, 1971

LEAP: Sam leaps in as Jesus Ortega, who is about to be electrocuted.

HEART STORY: Sam has to find proof that his character was the *sole* murderer in a case that has sent *two* men to Death Row. This will allow his "partner" to be exonerated.

KISS WITH HISTORY: None.

"A Hunting We Will Go," June 18, 1976

LEAP: Sam leaps in as bounty hunter Gordon O'Reilly who has been hired to bring a feisty female embezzler to justice.

HEART STORY: Sam realizes Diane embezzled the money to thwart an ongoing swindling scheme. He helps recover the money and exposes the sheriff and Diane's boss as the true criminals.

KISS WITH HISTORY: None.

"Heart of a Champion," July 23, 1955

LEAP: Sam leaps in as Terry Sammis, the newest member of a wrestling tag team composed of two brothers.

HEART STORY: Sam discovers his "brother" has a potentially fatal heart problem and saves his life by wrestling for him in the championship match.

KISS WITH HISTORY: None.

"Nuclear Family," October 26, 1962

LEAP: Sam leaps in as college student Eddie Elroy, who helps his brother sell atom bomb shelters during the height of the Cuban Missile Crisis.

HEART STORY: Sam has to help relieve the panic that will arise from the threat of a nuclear war and consume the Elroy family. In particular, he must stop his young nephew from accidentally shooting a neighbor whom he mistakes for an invading Russian soldier.

KISS WITH HISTORY: Cuban Missile Crisis.

"Shock Theater," October 3, 1954

LEAP: Sam leaps into the body of Sam Beederman, who is about to receive electroshock therapy.

HEART STORY: Sam's memory is distorted and he has trouble remembering who he is: Sometimes he believes he is different people from various past leaps. He can only make the leap back to normalcy by repeating the high voltage electroshock treatment that almost caused his death in the first place.

KISS WITH HISTORY: None.

FROM 1952 TO 1999: The Leaps in Chronological Order

With the exception of the pilot episode, which takes place in 1956 and leads off this section, what follows is a chronological listing of the leaps, with the original air dates for each episode. These synopses were originally prepared by a variety of network and studio publicity writers for weekly distribution to television critics around the country.

THE *QUANTUM LEAP* PILOT
Written by Donald P. Bellisario
Directed by David Hemmings

Sam wakes up in 1956 with a very pregnant wife, whom he doesn't know. He doesn't remember who he is, but quickly learns he's an Air Force test pilot with one child.

Sam decides to go along with all this until he can figure out what's going on. He's scheduled to fly the X-2, an experimental rocket plane. He should know how to fly one. After all, he is a pilot, isn't he? Then why can't he remember how to fly?

With the help of Al, the Observer who becomes visible to him for the first time, Sam does fly. He breaks Mach-3, thereby saving the real test pilot's life. He also saves the pilot's wife and newborn baby by applying his medical skills when she goes into premature labor. He then leaps to:

A ball park in Waco, Texas. Al tells Sam about the Quantum Leap experiment. In a poignant scene, Sam, as an adult, speaks to his father, who in Sam's present has been dead many years. Then Sam gets up to bat and strikes out, but the catcher misses the last ball allowing Sam to reach first base. The pitcher is the young Tom Seaver.

The pilot episode aired March 26, 1989.

"PLAY IT AGAIN, SEYMOUR,"
APRIL 14, 1953
Story by Tom Blomquist, Scott Shepherd, and Donald P. Bellisario
Teleplay by Scott Shepherd and Donald P. Bellisario
Directed by Aaron Lipstadt

Sam is Nick Allen, a cheap detective in an expensive suit, handcuffed and dragged off to jail by a cop after being arrested for a murder he didn't commit.

He befriends a newspaper boy, Seymour, who lives in a fantasy world, dreaming about becoming a writer of detective stories.

At the end of this moody episode, Sam gives inspiration to a young man who looks amazingly like Woody Allen.

Original airdate: May 17, 1989

"THE AMERICANIZATION OF MACHIKO,"
AUGUST 4, 1953
Written by Charlie Cofey
Directed by Gilbert Shilton

Sam steps off a bus in Norman Rockwell country. He is Charles Lee McKenzie, United States Navy, and he's in the small town of Oak Creek, along with a beautiful Japanese girl, Machiko. She is Charlie's wife. He hasn't told anyone that he has this new bride.

Prejudices still linger toward the Japanese and this hatred falls on Machiko. They can't escape it anywhere. Hardest to accept is the disdain from Charlie's mother. Sam must get this family together before he can leap.

Sam shows a new side in this story: his talent for language. He can speak Japanese.

Original airdate: October 11, 1989

"MIRROR IMAGE," AUGUST 8, 1953
Written by Donald P. Bellisario
Directed by James Whitmore, Jr.

Sam leaps into a tavern in Cokesburg, Pennsylvania, as himself on his day of birth. He befriends a wise bartender, Alberto Bellisario and a group of coal miners, on the series finale. [**Note:** For name clarification in this storyline, Al (Alberto) refers to Al the Bartender, and Al/The Observer will be referred to as the Observer.]

Sam enters Al's Place, a tavern full of local miners. He orders a drink from Al the bartender and catches a glimpse of a display behind the bar—photos and newspaper clippings of local soldiers. At the back of the bar, Sam spots a mirror and makes his way to see whom he has leapt into this time. To his surprise, Sam sees himself! His shock at the reflection is covered by a joke with the bartender, who laughs and shows Sam a picture of himself as a young and slender army lieutenant, which until lately was the only image he had of his now rounded body. Sam gets the newspaper only to find out it's August 8, 1953... the date of his birth. In the Waiting Room, the Observer and Gushie work frantically with Ziggy to locate Sam. Since it is empty, they figure that Sam is himself, somewhere in time.

Stawpah, a bar regular from Russia, is suspicious of Sam and asks him whether he is from State Liquor Control or a revenue agent. Sam, not really being certain himself, reaches for his wallet. The postman, a gnome-like character, arrives with the mail. The foul-smelling man reminds Sam of someone he knows. At the same time Al mentions that the guy's name is Gushie, just like Sam's head engineer. Stawpah is still convinced that Sam is pretending to be something he isn't, and Bartender Al tries to talk him out of his suspicions. Al comments that things could go wrong if he ever forgot anything. This statement comes within Sam's earshot, sending him into a flashback to the pilot season of *Quantum Leap*, with the Observer saying the same thing.

A miner named Tonchi enters the bar. To Sam's surprise, Tonchi looks and sounds just like Frank LaMatta from Sam's leap into "Jimmy LaMatta." Sam flashes back to his leap as "Jimmy," when he and Frank were playing around. Sam rushes over to hug Tonchi, thinking it's "Frank LaMatta." Tonchi doesn't recognize Sam and gives him a hard time. Later, Sam relaxes at a table and begins to watch "Captain Z-Ro" on television. A coal-dusted miner sits next to him, and Sam notices that he looks like "Captain Galaxy," from another leap. Sam asks if the miner's name is Moe Stein, like the actor who portrayed "Galaxy" in Sam's leap.

Sam tells Bartender Al that he knows another Al who uses the same sayings, questioning if all of these similarities are merely coincidence. The Observer must enter the Waiting Room to get a holographic lock across time with Sam's mind in order to locate him.

Sharp blasts of the mine whistle send everyone out of the bar and into the street. Smoke billows from the main shaft as a cage surfaces with choking miners emerging from the dense smoke. Tonchi and Frank are trapped, and the mine is filling with gas. Sam poses as a state safety inspector in order to convince Superintendent Collins to let him help go in after the brothers. More concerned about the mine blowing and costing the company money than about losing lives, Collins shuts down the mine.

Sam and Stawpah have a heart-to-heart talk about the brothers. Stawpah explains that if they aren't saved soon, they won't be alive much longer because of the poor conditions in the mine. He also explains that it was those conditions that caused his disabling arthritis.

Back at Al's Place, Sam ponders the situation and questions why he is there. Al asks Sam if he thinks he is there to save Tonchi and Pete. This shakes Sam, but he questions Al for knowing everything. Al's response is, "Only God knows everything. You don't think I'm God?" Stawpah enters and convinces Sam to play the safety inspector. Sam goes to the mine and fakes orders from the bureau in order to reopen the shaft. Miner Ziggy and Mutta go down to help.

In the Imaging Chamber, the Observer remembers it's Sam's birthday has Gushie run a check on all of Sam's birthdays.

Sam is at Al's Place again, explaining his relationship with the Observer. He recalls that they would do anything for each other. But Sam flashes back to his "M.I.A." leap, when he saved a police officer but couldn't prevent Beth, the Observer's ex-wife and only true love, from marrying another man. Tonchi, Pete, and the rest of the miners burst through the door, announcing drinks for everyone! Stawpah begins a toast and is engulfed in Quantum Blue light, and then he disappears. Confused, Sam questions what happened to Stawpah, and the miners jokingly ask for whatever Sam's drinking. He then realizes that Stawpah was a leaper too. Sam and Bearded Gushie begin talking about Gushie's old friend Steve (Stawpah) who just disappeared—except that Steve died twenty years ago.

Sam looks in the mirror again and sees the reflections of everyone in the bar except for Ziggy, Gushie, Tonchi, and Pete. He questions Al about why someone who is dead (Stawpah) can save the living, and Al replies, "That's the way it is." Al tells Sam that all along Sam has been leaping himself through time and that he controls his own destiny. Sam knows that he must right at least one more wrong before he can go home. He leaps to Beth to tell her to wait for the Observer, that he is alive, and he is coming home to her.

Written words that appear over black screen before the credits: Beth never remarried. She and Al/The Observer have four daughters and will celebrate their thirty-ninth wedding anniversary in June. Dr. Sam Beckett never returned home.

Original airdate: May 5, 1993

"A SINGLE DROP OF RAIN,"
SEPTEMBER 7, 1953
Written by Richard C. Okie
Directed by Virgil Vogel

Sam leaps into the body of Billy Beaumont, a twenty-seven-year-old traveling meteorologist and climatologist, who cons people into paying him to make rain and then runs off with their money.

As Sam leaps in, he has returned to a small Texas town to visit his mother. The town pleads with him to make it rain, but Al tells Sam no rain is expected for months.

Ralph, Billy's brother, is bitter that the town is being conned. Through Al, Sam discovers that Billy has been having an affair with Annie, Ralph's wife. Al learns that the real Billy took Annie with him when he fled town. Sam's mission is to keep Annie and Ralph together.

Sam prepares a solution to create rain clouds and decides that during a twon picnic he'll fly the solution up in helium balloons to release it high in the air.

As a fight over Annie breaks out between Sam/Billy and Ralph, Annie and Ralph reconcile, and raindrops begin to fall.

Original airdate: November 20, 1991

"MEMPHIS MELODY,"
JANUARY 4, 1954

SHOULD BE: JULY 3, 1954

Written by Robin Jill Bernheim
Directed by James Whitmore, Jr.

Sam leaps into young Elvis Presley. Sam/Elvis is in an auditorium during a rehearsal for the local talent show. Sue Anne Winters steps onstage and begins to sing. Overcome by nerves, she tries to regain her composure and starts again, only to exit the stage and run for the back of the auditorium. Sam/Elvis dashes to catch her on her way outside. Al/The Observer arrives to inform Sam that he has leapt in only two days before Elvis is to be discovered. He tells Sam/Elvis he is to help Sue Anne with her dreams of stardom. Sam/Elvis returns to the stage to do his rendition of "Dixie," while Al urges him on. The performance is only lukewarm and Red, Elvis's friend, questions Sam/Elvis's efforts.

Sam/Elvis and Red go to Taylor's diner, the local spot where Sue Anne and her sister Julie work. Sam/Elvis tells Sue Anne that she must keep reaching for her dreams of one day performing at the Opry. With that, Sam/Elvis begins to sing "Amazing Grace" and Sue Anne joins in and belts out an incredible rendition that brings the restaurant down. She is so excited she gives Sam/Elvis a huge hug. Red gets to chanting "more" and lifts Sue Anne on the front counter in front of Sam/Elvis

just as Frank Bigley, her fiancé, walks in. Frank reprimands Sue Anne for her unladylike behavior in public, lets Sam/Elvis and Red know what he thinks of them and warns them to keep away from her. Al tells Sam that, after this, Sue Anne abandons her dreams of performing to marry Frank and moves to Louisville to run the family business.

Sam/Elvis goes to Sun Records and makes a recording for his mother Gladys's birthday. It doesn't come out as planned, but Sam/Elvis tries to get Marion Keisker of Sun Records to play it for the studio owner, Mr. Phillips. He asks Marion to invite Phillips to the talent show, but she goes instead. Backstage, Sam/Elvis waits for his turn as Sue Anne walks into the spotlight. She begins to look sick with stage fright. Sam/Elvis rushes to her, and they bring down the house with a version of "Will the Circle Be Unbroken." Marion reaches them backstage and offers them both an audition with Phillips the next day. Frank and Sam/Elvis exchange jealous words and begin to fight. Sue Anne arrives to break it up.

Sam/Elvis goes to meet Sue Anne at the diner before their audition only to be told that she is leaving with Frank for Louisville. He races to her house to convince Sue Anne to stay for the audition with Phillips. She agrees to go, but they arrive to a closed studio. She is furious and leaves Sam/Elvis at the studio. Al explains that although Sue Anne didn't audition, the seed was planted with her for the future.

Al tells Sam/Elvis that he still has time to catch Phillips at the diner and get signed before the record head leaves for Nashville. He heads to Phillips's table in the diner and begs for five minutes. Phillips motions for some musicians in the next booth to come along with him and Sam/Elvis to the studio. Sam/Elvis breaks into "Blue Moon of Kentucky" and Phillips asks for one more song, telling Sam/Elvis to set up a session after his return from Nashville. Al tells Sam not to wait, Phillips cancels, and Elvis is never discovered. Sam/Elvis chases the label executive back to the diner, where he is finishing his meeting with a deejay. Standing in the middle of the diner, Sam grabs the crowd with an immortal version of "Baby, Let's Play House." Phillips is amazed by Sam/Elvis's "black voice" and the swooning girls, and signs him on the spot.

Sam goes to Sue Anne's to tell her he has set up an audition for her with Phillips now that he has been signed. She gets a contract, sings at the Grand Ole Opry and starts the first Elvis Presley Fan Club.

Original airdate: April 20, 1993

"SEA BRIDE," JUNE 3, 1954
Written by Deborah Pratt
Directed by Joe Napolitano

Traveling through time Sam appears in the stateroom of an ocean liner, thinking that perhaps he's John Paul Jones.

Suddenly, a door flies open and a beautiful woman, wearing a wedding dress that is barely pinned together, walks in and kisses him passionately. She then smacks him just as hard.

Her name is Catherine Farrington and she is about to get married, but not to Sam.

Sam has become Phillip Dumon, an international playboy and Catherine's ex-husband. Sam must stop the marriage in order to Quantum Leap. He must convince her to reunite with her ex-husband.

A highlight of this episode is a choreographed tango to biting dialogue. Much of the show was shot aboard the *Queen Mary* in Long Beach, California.

This episode received an Emmy nomination for Best Costume Design by Jean-Pierre Dorleac.

Original airdate: May 2, 1990

"POOL HALL BLUES," SEPTEMBER 4, 1954
Written by Randy Holland
Directed by Joe Napolitano

Sam is leaning over a pool table, under the harsh glow of an overhead lamp. A woman is singing the blues in the distance. Sam slowly raises his eyes and then his cue, realizing that he is in a high-stakes game of pool and has to shoot. He nervously takes aim at the eight ball and hits it with too much force, missing the pocket by more than a foot. Sam gulps in dismay.

Sam is Charlie "Black Magic" Waters, a black man and famous pool hustler. Sam won't Quantum Leap unless he can help a woman keep her club open, winning it for her in a pool game. The only problem is that Sam doesn't play pool.

Scott Bakula has a showcase for his singing and piano playing in this tender episode.

Original airdate: March 14, 1990

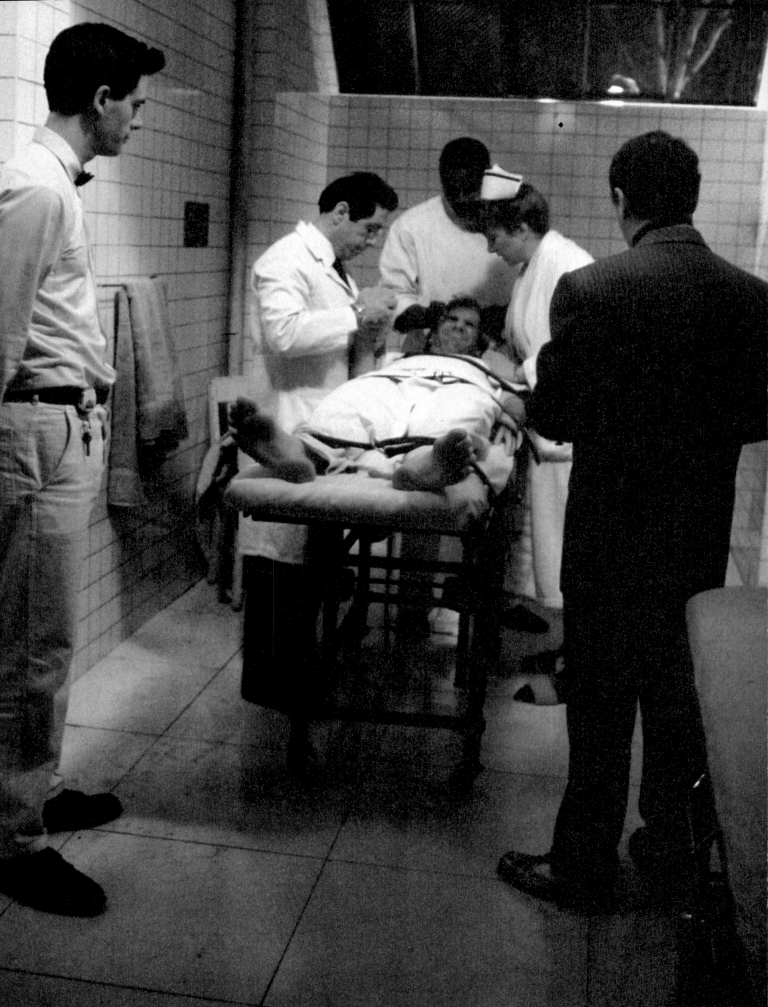

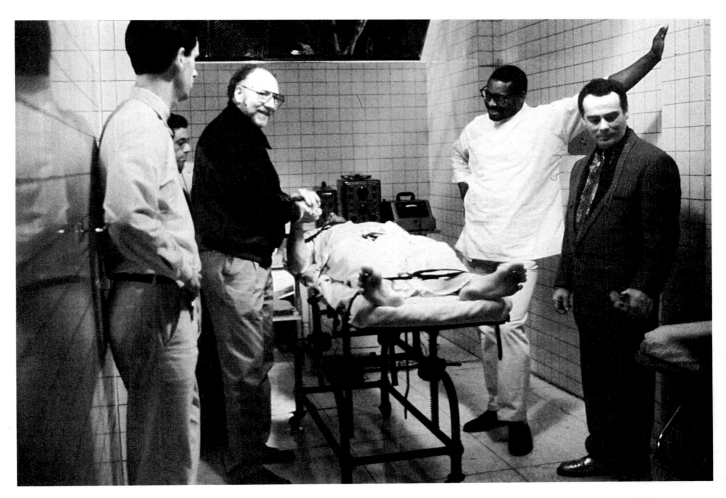

"SHOCK THEATER," OCTOBER 3, 1954
Written by Deborah Pratt
Directed by Joe Napolitano

Sam finds himself in a straightjacket in the middle of a therapy room. Two attendants are holding him down. The windows are barred. Sam must be in some sort of institution, strapped down for shock treatment.

Sam is Sam Beederman—hospitalized for acute depression.

The shock hits Sam hard. Al thinks that he has lost Sam. The only way to get Sam back is to go through another shock treatment.

In this season-ender, Scott Bakula reprises some of the best characters from previous episodes. He won the Golden Globe Award as Best Actor in a Drama Series for this episode.

Original airdate: May 22, 1991

"HEART OF A CHAMPION," JULY 23, 1955
Written by Tommy Thompson
Directed by Joe Napolitano

Sam is watching a large man in red wrestling tights and boots get clobbered in the ring.

The man moves toward Sam and reaches out to tag him to enter the ring. Sam is part of a "Russian" tag team!

Sam finds he's not really Russian at all. He is involved in one of the lowest forms of entertainment—professional wrestling.

Sam discovers that his "brother" has a potentially fatal heart disease and must stop him from going for the championship match.

Original airdate: May 8, 1991

"COLOR OF TRUTH," AUGUST 8, 1955
Written by Deborah Pratt
Directed by Mike Vejar

Finding himself in a Southern diner, Sam takes a seat at the friendly counter and everything stops. Everyone stares.

Sam looks around and then into the mirror. He sees a black man of about seventy staring back at him. He is Jessie Tyler, a driver for a rich Southern woman known as Miz Melny.

Sam has sparked a controversy by sitting down at an all-white diner and a few men are going to make sure that it doesn't happen again.

When Al pops in, he talks about the marches in Selma, where he demonstrated. But Sam isn't here to start the civil-rights movement.

Miz Melny will get hit by a train while in the car. Al's not sure if Sam will be with her at the time. But, he is her driver.

This episode was the first in which Sam Quantum Leaped into a person of a different race. Deborah Pratt won the Women in Film award for Best Writing for a Drama Series for this episode.

Original airdate: May 3, 1989

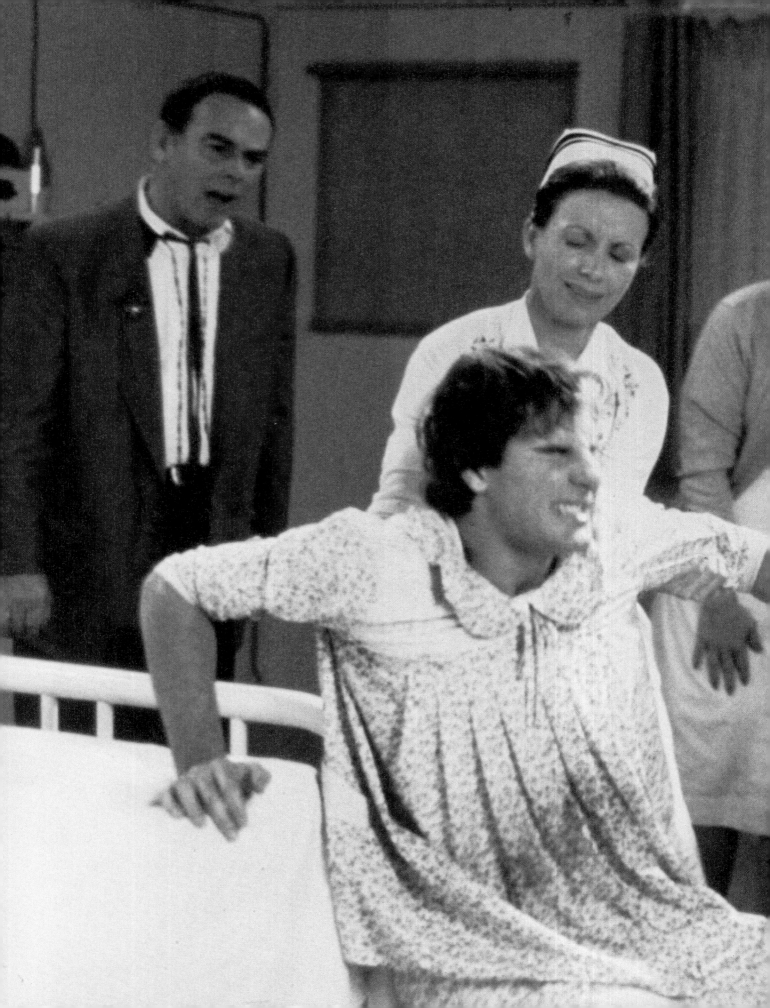

"ONE LITTLE HEART," AUGUST 8, 1955
(Part One of a Trilogy also including June 14, 1966 and July 28, 1978)
Written by Deborah Pratt
Directed by James Whitmore, Jr.

Bart Aider is found dead in the forest. The autopsy shows that he died of heart failure, but he also suffered a severe blow to the head. Sam/Clayton Fuller's ten-year-old daughter Abagail was the last person to see him alive when he threatened to strike her in a dispute over a locket. Two years earlier the same locket was fought over by Abagail and Bart's daughter Violet, just before Violet disappeared, leaving behind a blood-stained sweater. A pack of wild dogs was blamed for her disappearance. But Bart's widow, crazed with grief, believes Abagail murdered her daughter—and now her husband. Ziggy has found a record of Clayton and Abagail dying the next day, when their house catches on fire. Al warns Sam/Clayton that Leta may be the arsonist.

Sam learns that Clayton's wife Laura is alive and in a mental asylum. He also finds out from Will Kinman, a teenager who helps around the police station, that Laura's mother killed all her children except Laura, then took her own life. The simple folk of Potterville believe the family has been cursed since the 1700s.

While Sam goes to see Laura, Leta goes after Abagail, accusing her repeatedly of killing Violet for the locket and demanding it back. Sam and Al rush back to town in the nick of time to rescue Abagail from the Clayton house, set ablaze by the crazed Leta. He sees the ghostly figure of Laura and is mesmerized. As flames engulf him, Sam is enveloped in a blaze of Quantum blue.

Original airdate: November 17, 1992

"BILLY JEAN," NOVEMBER 15, 1955
Written by Deborah Pratt
Directed by James Whitmore, Jr.

Sam is being raced on a gurney through a hospital corridor. A woman is holding his hand and telling him he is going to be all right. Sam is in *unbearable pain*.

He checks himself for blood, but can't seem to find an injury. Instead, Sam is a single, very pregnant sixteen-year-old.

The news looks grim. Al tells Sam that unless he can leap out of there, which he must do before final labor, the baby could end up in the future.

Sam has to reconcile with the girl's father and ensure that the baby will have a good life with a single parent before he can Leap.

In "real" history, the girl gave up the baby for adoption and spent her life looking for the child.

To work on the character, Bakula wore a "pregnancy suit" that simulates the weight distribution of a pregnant woman.

AKA:
8½ MONTHS

Original airdate: March 6, 1991

45

"HOW THE TESS WAS WON," AUGUST 5, 1956
**Written by Deborah Arakelian
Directed by Ivan Dixon**

Sam finds himself in the muck and mire of a pig sty, holding a piglet that is squealing with excitement.

He is in Texas, on a ranch called the Riata—fifty thousand acres, owned by Tess, the toughest young woman in the state. Sam is Patrick Young, the local veterinarian.

Tess's father complains that she doesn't know how to be a woman. She challenges him to a bet: She will marry Sam if he can out-rope, out-ride, and "out-cowboy" her for a week.

Sam is not too keen on this idea. Al advises that in order to leap he has to get the two married. The actual vet is really in love with her, but Tess is completely unaware of his feelings. It doesn't look hopeful.

Sam continually carries around the piglet. One of the ranchhands, Buddy Holly, keeps singing a song he is writing. Sam helps him compose... "Piggy Sue."

Original airdate: April 14, 1989

"GHOST SHIP," AUGUST 13, 1956
Written by Paris Qualles and Donald P. Bellisario
Directed by Anita Addison

Sam leaps into Eddie Brackett, private plane copilot flying Grant and Michelle Cutter, rich young newlyweds, to Bermuda in a converted Grumman Goose with seasoned pilot Dan Cooper.

The compass goes out of control as they enter the Bermuda Triangle, so Cooper turns back.

Al reports that Michelle will die of a burst appendix if Eddie doesn't persuade Cooper to fly through the Bermuda Triangle, instead of making the longer trip back.

Al also discloses that in World War II Cooper lost his crew and spent eight days at sea in the Triangle before being rescued—none of which he can remember.

As they head into the Triangle, on a course plotted by Ziggy, Cooper begins to relive his last mission. Sam improvises a saline IV solution when Michelle's appendix bursts. After a lightning strike, as they limp in on one engine, Cooper recalls that he and his crew were also struck by lightning on that last mission and that he was picked up by the *USS Cyclops,* which was torpedoed a week later. Al reports that the *Cyclops* disappeared in the Triangle in 1918.

Original airdate: March 4, 1992

"LEAPING OF THE SHREW," SEPTEMBER 27, 1956
Written by Richard C. Okie and Robin Jill Bernheim
Directed by Alan Levi

Sam finds himself in the Aegean Sea, in the body of deckhand Nikos Stathatos, trying to save spoiled rich girl Vanessa Foster (played by Brooke Shields) from drowning, just after the yacht on which he was working explodes and sinks. Vanessa and her fiancé had chartered the yacht for their wedding voyage. When Sam/Nikos spots a rubber raft nearby, they clamber into it and he is able to retrieve her wardrobe trunk and lash it onto the raft. Albert reports that Vanessa's fiancé is safe, but the raft is way off course; Sam has changed history, and Vanessa and Nikos are never found.

Sam makes a sail out of Vanessa's wedding dress, and they eat seaweed and toothpaste. In conversation, Vanessa defends her busy, powerful father, and Sam realizes that her decisions have always been made for her family, not for herself. The next morning, they wake up on a deserted island. Al informs Sam that there is plenty of natural food to be found; that there is no dangerous wildlife; and that no one else will set foot on the island for nine years. Al also tells Sam that the real Nikos, who is waiting in the Imaging Chamber, is seriously in love with Vanessa. The fun and games in a fresh water pool turn into a long, serious kiss for the two until Vanessa accuses Sam of trying to seduce her. Continuing their search for food, Vanessa proves herself to be resourceful, a good berry picker and clam digger, and she shares her food with Sam. When a ship appears on the horizon, Sam vainly attempts to signal. Little does he know that Vanessa does not want them to be found!

Al's explanation to Sam is that Vanessa was drawn to Nikos before the ship's explosion, which she actually caused. She had followed Nikos to the yacht's engine room and threw her cigarette into a bin with greasy rags. Now, alone on the island with him, she realizes she wants to be with him, not with the man her family picked for her. When another ship appears on the horizon, she admits to not wanting to be rescued. Ziggy reports that Vanessa and Nikos will be found in nine years—with six children!

Original airdate: September 29, 1992

"RETURN OF THE EVIL LEAPER,"
OCTOBER 8, 1956
Written by Richard C. Okie
Directed by Harvey Laidman

Sam leaps in spread-eagled on the hood of a drag-racing car. When it screeches to a stop throwing Sam/"Midnight Marauder" to the ground, Mike Hammond, president of the Chi Kappa fraternity, rushes over and tears off the costume to reveal Sam/Arnold to the initiation crowd. This evokes a fight, and the cops arrive to break up the gathering. The Eastern State University dean puts all Chi Kappas on probation for hazing, and Mike wants revenge. Jack Swenson, Arnold's roommate and a third generation Chi Kappa pledge, is furious with Sam/Arnold and demands that the "caped crusader" stop. When Mike and fraternity brother Frank meet up with Sam/Arnold, words are exchanged, and Dawn Taylor, Mike's girlfriend, arrives. We see the familiar red Quantum light and see that Dawn is really Alia, the "evil leaper." A spark ignites between Alia/Dawn and Sam/Arnold. Neither Sam nor Alia know of each other's presence.

Mike and Alia/Dawn plot public humiliation against Sam/Arnold. Sam/Arnold studies for a science final and Alia/Dawn apologizes for Mike's behavior. She asks for midterm help, perhaps a study date. Sam/Arnold agrees to help her, if she will convince Mike to find safer ways of initiation. While in the Waiting Room, Al and Dr. Beeks, the psychologist, try to help Arnold realize it is not his responsibility to protect innocent people and that he must quit his suicidal behavior. Arnold's destiny must be changed in order for Sam to leap. Alia waits for her study date with Zoey, her observer, when their handlink relays that Sam/Arnold is at Road's End messing up her mission. Alia rushes to Road's End, as the crowd moves in on Sam/Arnold for wrecking another initiation. Sam calls for Al's help and Zoey and Alia realize Arnold is Dr. Beckett.

Zoey tells Alia that she and Sam cannot touch; Sam will know it's her. Alia must make certain that she kills Arnold, with no foul-ups. Mike and Alia/Dawn get into an argument and Sam/Arnold walks into it. Alia is setting Sam up. Mike challenges Sam/Arnold to a race and leaves. Sam/Arnold reaches for Alia/Dawn, and with a Quantum burst, they see who they really are for the first time. They kiss, then she tells him of her mission to make sure Arnold dies. The only way Sam can leap is to insure that Arnold doesn't die now and that Alia leaps with him. At Road's End, Sam wins Mike's challenge and he and Alia leap together.

Original airdate: February 23, 1993

SHOULD BE:
February 16, 1993

SHOULD BE:
November 2, 1956

"UNCHAINED," NOVEMBER 11, 1956
Written by Paris Qualles
Directed by Michael Watkins

Sam finds himself serving time on a chain gang as Chance Cole, a petty thief.

He's yanked off a truck by Boone, to whom he is shackled, as Boone attempts to escape, and the two succeed in dodging Boss Cooley and his Doberman. Sam saves Boone's life, but they're captured and Boone is thrown into a punishment pit.

Al reports that Chance's sentence was nine months, but he's been in jail for over two years. According to Ziggy, Boone is innocent of his crime. As Sam tells Boone about the real culprit, Jake Wiles, he's caught and tossed into the pit too.

Boone, raised by his Indian grandmother, has the soul of a poet and, when he overhears Sam talking to Al, he thinks that Al is a spirit.

Boss Cooley and jake Wiles are in league. Cooley kills Wiles and then Cooley himself gets killed while chasing Sam and Boone. Al reports that both men disapear into society and that the road prison is closed.

Original airdate: November 27, 1991

"CURSE OF PHTAH-HOTEP," MARCH 2, 1957
Written by Chris ruppenthal
Directed by Joe Mapolitano

SHOULD BE:
PTAH-HOTEP

Sam leaps into the body of Dale Conway, a professor of archeology, who is exploring the tomb of Ptah-Hotep in Egypt with Ginny Will, an attractive colleague. The tomb has a curse on it, and death has come to those who've disturbed it before.

Al tells Sam that Dale and Ginny disappear on a dig and he must prevent this from happening.

Dr. Mustafa, head of antiquities at the Luxor Museum, arrives at the site. Workers begin dying mysteriously.

With a sandstorm approaching, Sam/Dale discovers the mummy, which has a diamond "heart." An explosion rocks the burial chamber. Al and Ginny are trapped and Al tells them they have only two days of air.

Sam/Dale reads the hieroglyphs on the scarab and follows its directions, pushing at places on the wall to cause it to move and allow them escape. Outside, Mustafa waits with a gun.

When Sam knocks his gun away, he and Ginny escape, but Mustafa is trapped. San/Dale tells him how to follow the hieroglyphs to get out but Nustafa gets killed by the mummy before he can escape.

Original airdate: April 22, 1992

49

"A LEAP FOR LISA," JUNE 22, 1957
Written by Donald P. Bellisario
Directed by James Whitmore, Jr.

Sam leaps into Al as a young naval pilot, then known as Bingo. He's about to be tried for the murder of his commander's wife, Marci Riker, who had sexually initiated every pilot in the squadron with her husband's knowledge.

Sam learns that Chip Ferguson is Bingo's best friend and was with him on the night of Marci's murder; he also finds out that Lisa, a nurse with whom Bingo is in love, wants to confess and clear him of the accusation.

Sam/Bingo won't let her confess and Lisa dies in a car accident. Sam realizes that he didn't leap in to save Lisa, but to prove Bingo's innocence, but everything he does seems to bring Bingo closer to a guilty verdict and execution.

As Ziggy's odds of conviction approach 100 percent, Al disappears and even the memory of him fades from Sam's mind.

Al is replaced in Sam's mind by Edward St. John, who reports that Bingo's Corvette could prove his innocence. Sam searches the car and finds a cigar butt, at which point St. John reverts back to Al.

The cigar was Chip's. He loved Marci, but killed her accidently. Al returns to theChamber and succeeds in sending his young self back into Sam/Bingo with instructions to keep Chip away from Marci, thereby saving both Marci and Lisa.

Original airdate: May 20, 1992

"SO HELP ME, GOD," JULY 29, 1957
Written by Deborah Pratt
Directed by Andy Cadiff

Sam leaps into Leonard Dancey, a Southern lawyer in the sleepy town of Twelve Oaks Parish. The judge asks him how his client pleads—guilty or not guilty—to murder.

Sam turns to look at his client: She is Lila, a beautiful, if simple, young black woman who clutches a silver cross that hangs around her neck. Sam looks closely in her eyes. He then turns and pleads, "Not guilty."

Sam did not realize that a bargain had been made and she would have gotten twenty years. Sam has now angered the judge, who will pursue a first-degree murder charge and the death penalty.

Sam knows in his heart that she isn't guilty of killing Houston Cotter, her employer, but if he doesn't find the truth, Lila will die in the electric chair.

Deborah Pratt won the Angel Award for writing for this episode.

Original airdate: November 29, 1989

"FUTURE BOY," OCTOBER 6, 1957
Written by Tommy Thompson
Directed by Michael Switzer

Sam sits in front of some kind of control panel as the voice of Captain Galaxy tells him to activate the time machine.

Sam notices lights and cue cards. He is part of a local kiddie show. Sam is Kenny, better known as Future Boy, sidekick to Captain Galaxy, a failed actor who needs to earn a living.

Sam eventually learns that Moe Stein (Captain Galaxy) has attempted to create his own time machine in the basement of his house. Each time he attempts to move into the future, he puts his own life in serious danger. His daughter wants him committed. Sam must stop her from putting her own father into a mental institution.

Sam, as Future Boy, changes his own history by giving himself the idea for Quantum Leaping.

Original airdate: March 13, 1991

"GOOD NIGHT, DEAR HEART," NOVEMBER 9, 1957
Written by Paul Brown
Directed by Chris Welch

Sam stares at a heart-shaped locket. Inscribed on the back are the words "My love, forever," in German. Sam gets an eerie feeling about this locket. The owner is dead. Sam wonders why it's in his possession until he finds he is a mortician.

Sam becomes obsessed with the death of this woman. All the pieces to her puzzle don't quite fit. She supposedly committed suicide. But did she?

Original airdate: March 7, 1990

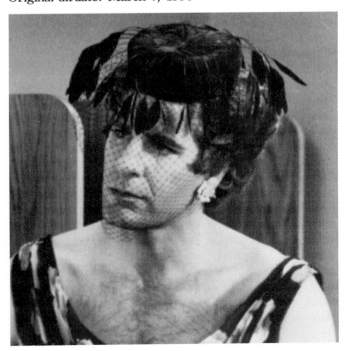

"THE LAST GUNFIGHTER," NOVEMBER 28, 1957
Story by Sam Rolff and Chris Ruppenthal
Teleplay by Chris Ruppenthal
Directed by Joe Napolitano

Sam leaps into eighty-two-year-old Tyler Means as he stages a shootout for tourists in the town of Coffin, Arizona.

Means as a young man single-handedly cleaned up the town by shooting the four infamous Claggett brothers. Now, a Hollywood writer wants the rights to Means's story.

Al says that Means will be killed tomorrow at noon by the elderly cowboy who will ride up and challenge him to a gunfight. That old cowboy, Pat Knight, was the one who really killed the Claggetts.

Means's grandson, Stevie, is afraid that his grandfather *is* a liar and will be killed; he straps on Means's six-shooter and goes to face Knight himself.

Sam rushes to the town saloon, takes the gunbelt from Stevie, faces Knight, and outdraws him.

Al reports that the Hollywood contract gets signed, along with financial security for daughter-in-law Lucy and Stevie. Sam/Tyler arranges a consulting position on the television series for Knight.

Original airdate: February 5, 1992

"A TALE OF TWO SWEETIES," FEBRUARY 25, 1958
Written by Robin Jill Bernheim
Directed by Chris Hibler

Sam/Mary exits from an airplane and is met by two wives and two sets of children. He quickly tells one family he'll meet them at the hotel and the other that he'll meet them at the movies. While at the movies, Sam/Marty is beaten up by Gus and Vic, to whom he owes money from gambling on the horse races. Both Rachel and Ellen, Sam/Marty's two wives, ban him from his families because he is always selling furniture and jewelry for gambling money. He has even gone so far as to take money from the children. Ellen and Rachel meet at the beauty parlor and both respond when the receptionist calls for "Mrs. Ellroy."

Vic and Gus arrive to get the money that bigamist Sam/Marty owes him, but he convinces them to allow him to make one more bet. Sam/Marty picks the winning horse and clears his debts. He is then confronted by both Ellen and Rachel. He tells them the truth. At first, they fight for him, then they realize he is no good and both decide to leave him. Al tells Sam that Rachel goes on to marry a doctor and Ellen becomes a marriage counselor and eventually remarries. Marty cleans up his act and starts a new life.

Original airdate: January 5, 1993

"IT'S A WONDERFUL LEAP," MAY 10, 1958
Story by Paul Brown and Dani Alexandra
Teleplay by Dani Alexandra
Directed by Paul Brown

Sam leaps into the body of Max Greenman, a New York cab driver. He unexpectedly hits a woman and, with her lying under his cab, he fears she's dead. But she gets up and introduces herself as Angela, announces that she's fine and that she's Max's guardian angel. Inside the cab, Angela tells Sam/Max she can see Al.

Al lets Sam know that Angela gets shot in a robbery, but because she's an angel, the bullet passes through her and hits Max in the head, just as he is about to win a $20,000 medallion from the cab company, currently in the hands of his rival, Frank.

Suddenly, an armed mugger forces Sam/Max out of the cab. The mugger shoots Angela, who falls to the ground. When the mugger flees, Angela gets up, saying that angels don't die.

But Sam/Max loses the medallion because of the robbery. Al tells Sam that Lenny, Max's father, will shoot the cab-company owner if Max doesn't get the medallion.

Lenny takes Frank hostage, but Sam persuades him to give up his gun. Al reveals that Frank set up the robbery, so Max wouldn't get the medallion.

The medallion is awarded to Max and he and his father start their own cab company with the money.

Original airdate: April 1, 1992

"KILLIN' TIME," JUNE 18, 1958
Written by Tommy Thompson
Directed by Michael Watkins

Sam finds himself holding eight-year-old Becky and her pretty mother Carol hostage in their house. A news report on the television tells him he is Leon Stiles, a killer on the run. The police, led by Sheriff John Hoyt, have the house surrounded. Meanwhile, in the Imaging Chamber the confused but desperate and dangerous Stiles steals a gun from a Quantum Military police officer and aims it at Al, demanding a car for escape. The MPs are puzzled because they see Sam and not Stiles. Sam is about to cut his hostages free when Al intervenes and explains that he must continue holding them because they are his only insurance against being killed by Sheriff Hoyt, whose daughter was murdered by Stiles. Originally Hoyt shot Stiles as he left the house, because he held a gun, and later Hoyt was fired because witnesses claimed that Stiles was unarmed and was willing to surrender. Hoyt wound up drinking himself to death a few years afterward. Al tells Sam he must stop Stiles from being killed.

Sam attempts to convince Carol and Becky that he is not Stiles by telling them about the Quantum Leap project. He explains that he is a doctor and has the ability to travel in time and leap into others' bodies while retaining his own spirit. When a television news broadcast claims that Stiles is illiterate, Sam asks Carol, who is putting herself through medical school, to test his medical knowledge to prove the truth of his story.

Since Al is tracking Stiles, Gooshie appears in Al's place to tell Sam that Hoyt will soon storm into the house and shoot him, but Becky will also be killed in the crossfire. Sam/Stiles sends Becky out of the house to save her life. In the meantime, Stiles solicits a hooker, and while in her bedroom, he aims his gun at her. Just in time, Al finds Stiles, jumps in with his gun drawn, and gets shot down. Stiles takes Al's handlink, believing Al is dead. Al fires a tranquilizer dart into Stiles, who is then taken to the Waiting Room. When Hoyt storms the house, Carol stands in front of Sam, shielding him and saving him from being shot. At this point Sam leaps.

Original airdate: October 20, 1992

"MISS DEEP SOUTH," JUNE 7, 1958
Written by Tommy Thompson
Directed by Chris Welch

Sam sits on a bus waving good-bye to a woman who must be his mother. She jumps aboard and places a sash over his shoulder, which reads "Miss Sugar Belle."

Sam is Darlene Monty, a beauty-pageant contestant. Sam has to endure the humiliation of learning to walk, talk and dance like a Southern belle. He also has to wear a bathing suit.

Sam becomes roommates with another contestant, Connie Duncan, who has high hopes of a career in Hollywood. The pageant photographer tells her that he can get her a screen test if she poses nude for him.

Sam attempts to stop her, knowing these pictures will be used for blackmail, but he is too late. Sam and Al must stop the photographer from releasing the photos.

In this episode Sam and Al do a hilarious Carmen Miranda number together.

Original airdate: November 2, 1990

"REBEL WITHOUT A CLUE,"
SEPTEMBER 1, 1958
Written by Randy Holland and Paul Brown
Directed by James Whitmore, Jr.

Winding around the curves of Pacific Coast Highway is a group of bikers. Someone is riding with them who doesn't have quite the expertise of the others.

It's Sam, who swerves to avoid a collision with the others and tumbles down a dirt embankment, with the motorcycle right behind him.

Sam is Shane "Funny Bone" Thomas, a biker and the clown for this group of rebels.

Sam has to prevent Becky, the gang leader's girlfriend, from being murdered by her abusive old man, and attempts to talk her into following her dream of becoming a successful novelist.

He encounters and asks Jack Kerouac for help.

Original airdate: November 30, 1990

"LEAPING WITHOUT A NET,"
NOVEMBER 18, 1958
Written by Tommy Thompson
Directed by Chris Welch

Sam is upside down and swinging. An eighteen-year-old girl is looking at him from a platform high above the ground. She tells him not to tense up.

He suddenly realizes he is swinging in the catcher's position as she dives from the platform. Sam is supposed to catch her in midair!

Sam is Victor Panzini, a member of a family trapeze act. The family is torn apart and the act is about to be.

Sam must reconcile father and son and restore the act to the way it used to be. All this without a net!

Original airdate: March 28, 1990

"STAND-UP," APRIL 30, 1959
Written by Deborah Pratt
Directed by Michael Zinberg

Sam becomes singer Davey Parker, half of Parker and MacKay, a nightclub act.

When Sam leaps in in the middle of the act, he ruins the routine, but Frankie, an attractive waitress with a crush on MacKay, jumps in with her own impromptu jokes, saves the act, and the three of them head off to Las Vegas.

Al reports that after opening night Mack will die. Sam must prevent Mack from quitting the act and must keep the Vegas hotelier, Carlo De Gorio, from killing Mack to get Frankie for himself.

Just before the show, DeGorio gives Frankie a fur coat, and in a rage, Mack hits him, then storms out.

Frankie convinces Mack that it's he whom she loves. He returns, the three of them do a great show, and Sam/ Davey convinces DeGorio not to kill Mack.

Original airdate: May 13, 1992

"GOOD MORNING, PEORIA,"
SEPTEMBER 9, 1959
Written by Chris Ruppenthal
Directed by Michael Zinberg

With the sounds of Little Richard's "Tutti-Frutti" coming to an end, Sam finds himself at the controls at a small radio station.

He's Howlin' Chick Howell, the baddest D.J. in Peoria, who has gone through twelve jobs in the last year.

Rachel Porter has just taken over the station after her father passed away, and the town is in an uproar because she won't stop playing the "devil's music," rock and roll.

Al tells Sam that he has to save the station for Rachel by making it number one. The only way to do that is by playing rock and roll.

Chubby Checker appears as himself trying to get his demo played. Sam is excited and starts singing, "Come on baby, let's do the Twist." Chubby asks Sam if he can use that in his act. Sam has just invented the Twist.

Original airdate: November 8, 1989

"GOODBYE NORMA JEAN," APRIL 4, 1960
Written by Richard C. Okie
Directed by Chris Hibler

Sam/Dennis hires Barbara Whitmore as an assistant for Marilyn Monroe. Al tells Sam/Dennis that Marilyn is expected to commit suicide in four days, and that the cause of death is listed as barbiturate overdose, mixed with champagne. Marilyn goes out in public "dressed down," so she's not recognized, and calls herself Norma Jean Baker. Barbara dresses up as a brunette version of Marilyn, even adding the facial mole. As Marilyn calls for her, she quickly changes. Marilyn tells Barbara to get Peter Lawford on the phone and RSVP to a party that Marilyn encourages Barbara to attend as her guest. Al tells Sam/Dennis that Lawford is legendary for booze, sex, and dope parties. At the soirée, Marilyn and Lawford disappear. Minutes later, he's calling for a doctor because Marilyn has passed out and is unresponsive. Sam/Dennis revives her and Lawford admits to giving her pills.

Marilyn gives Sam/Dennis a long, sensual kiss to thank him. She tries to seduce him, but he brushes her off, something no man has ever done before. Sam/Dennis reveals to Marilyn that Barbara had been lying about her background all along. She's really an actress named Mary Joe Vermullen, and not a young widow from Ohio. Marilyn doesn't want to hear the truth and fires Sam/Dennis. John Huston is waiting for Marilyn at a rehearsal, when Barbara shows up to stand in for her. Clark Gable appears as the leading man and finds himself falling in love with Barbara. Nevertheless, Sam/Dennis goes to Marilyn's house, where she's curled up in bed with a massive hangover. He forces her into the shower and pours coffee down her throat. Gable begins to dance with Barbara, and Marilyn suddenly appears and cuts in. Al tells Sam/Dennis that he has saved her life, and she stars in her last film.

Original airdate: March 2, 1993

"HONEYMOON EXPRESS," APRIL 27, 1960
Written by Donald P. Bellisario
Directed by Aaron Lipstadt

What sets this story apart is that, in the "present," Al has to make the case for supporting the Project to Congress, or funds will be cut and Sam will be lost forever, jumping through time.

Also, this is the only double leap in one episode. First, he's a fireman up a tree, trying to rescue a kitten.

Al tells him that it's 1957, Sam leaps for the cat, falls to the ground; the cat lands on all fours on his chest, and Sam Quantum Leaps to...

A fast-moving passenger train. He is kissing a beautiful young woman.

Sam is Tom McBride, on the Honeymoon Express. He's athletic, handsome, a lieutenant with the NYPD, and an unfortunate soul who is missing his own honeymoon with his bride, Diane.

Diane is kidnapped by her ex-husband, an arms smuggler from France. Sam has to save Diane from the clutches of her ex-husband, as well as save himself.

Al fights for the Project, and Sam fights for Diane.

Original airdate: September 20, 1989

"THE WRONG STUFF," JANUARY 24, 1961
Written by Paul Brown
Directed by Joe Napolitano

Sam leaps into the body of Bobo, a chimp in a space program. Dr. Leslie Ashton is a young vet who studies animal behavior and must prevent her associate, Dr. Winger, from killing chimps in his crash-helmet research.

When he finds himself in a space capsule, Sam tries to explain to Ashton that he is not a chimpanzee, but grunts are the only sounds he can make.

Al says that Bobo will die of massive head injuries. A military officer shoots Cory, an amorous female chimp, with a dart that temporarily paralyzes her. Al learns that Cory will die of head injuries.

Sam uses sign language to convey to Ashton that Cory was taken away to be used in Winger's experiments. While the doctors argue, Bobo frees himself, and he and Cory flee.

Winger chases the two chimps, but when the doctor falls into a lake, Bobo saves him, and Winger realizes that chimpanzees have humanlike qualities.

As Sam leaps out, Al learns that Winger develops a computer that simulates crashes and that Ashton opens a sanctuary for chimps. Cory and Bobo become parents.

Original airdate: November 6, 1991

"CAMIKAZI KID," JUNE 6, 1961
Written by Paul Brown
Directed by Alan J. Levi

Sam finds himself driving a speeding car. He slams on the brakes and checks out his face in the sideview mirror. He is a skinny, seventeen-year-old member of a "normal" all-American family. His older sister is about to get married.

Al reveals that there is little future for the sister's marriage. Sam also notices she's bruised.

The entire family is in denial over this, and Sam has to find a way of stopping this doomed marriage before it starts.

While Sam is in the bathroom with Al at the wedding dinner, a young black boy comes in. Sam invents the "Moonwalk" for a young Michael Jackson.

Original airdate: May 10, 1989

"SOUTHERN COMFORTS," AUGUST 4, 1961
Written by Tommy Thompson
Directed by Chris Ruppenthal

Sam sits in front of a birthday cake on which fifty candles are lit. He blows them out.

Applause breaks out as the lights go on and Sam is surrounded by women. One woman is ready to give Sam his gift. As she grabs him below the waist, Sam's voice jumps a few octaves with a variation on his familiar, "Whoa, boy."

Sam is the owner of a brothel and is romantically pursued by the madame. Sam has to help the madame's pregnant cousin escape her abusive husband.

Original airdate: April 4, 1991

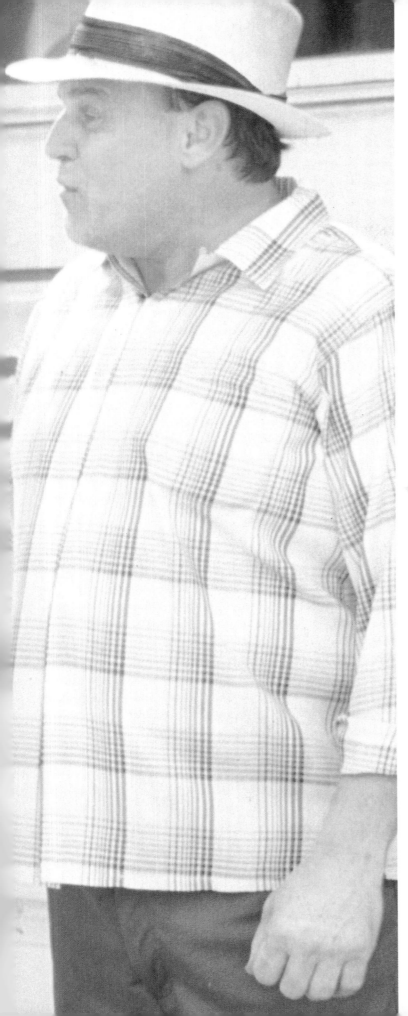

"PLAY BALL," AUGUST 6, 1961
Written by Tommy Thompson
Directed by Joe Napolitano

Sam leaps into Lester "Doc" Fuller, pitcher for the Galveston Mustangs, a minor-league team.

Doc left the majors after accidentally killing a player with a fastball; now, he's befriending Chucky, a promising young pitcher with a drinking problem.

When Chucky tells Sam his father was once a famous ballplayer, Al and Ziggy locate the father, down-and-outer Warren Monroe.

Reminded of when he first met Al, Sam realizes that Chucky's drinking is out of control. When Sam and Al find Chucky passed out in his girlfriend's bedroom, her mother, who owns the team, kicks both Chucky and Doc off the squad.

An Immigration Department raid leaves the team with only eight players, so the owner relents, letting Chucky pitch. He, in turn, gives his chance to Sam/Doc.

Sam pitches a great game, but deliberately pulls himself out of the game with a "sore arm." He turns the pitching over to Chucky and moves into the outfield, where he catches the last out, clinching the championship.

Afterward, a big-league scout offers both Chucky and Sam/Doc contracts, and Chucky is reunited with his father.

Original airdate: September 25, 1991

71

"WHAT PRICE GLORIA?"
OCTOBER 16, 1961
Written by Deborah Pratt
Directed by Alan J. Levi

Sam literally leaps into hot water...a bubble bath.

His roommate, Gloria Collins, walks in wearing a bra and panties and talks about the promotion they are both up for. When Sam looks in the mirror, Samantha Stormer stares back—naked and soaking wet.

This is the first episode in which Sam leaps into a woman. Sam, an executive secretary at National Motor Company in Detroit, has to manage wearing high heels and getting hit on by men. This is too strange for him to deal with.

Sam learns that Gloria has been fooling around with B. J. Wright, the company's new vice-president of development. She is waiting for him to leave his wife. B. J. not only didn't tell Gloria of his promotion, he made Sam/Samantha his secretary. It isn't enough that Sam is being pursued by the mailroom boy, but now he is also being propositioned by his own boss.

Al is a little worried; even he finds Sam attractive. When Sam rejects B.J.'s advances, B.J. turns back to Gloria and tells her he's going to leave his wife to marry her.

Al informs Sam that in the real history, there was never a wedding, and if he (Sam) doesn't help, Gloria will commit suicide.

"This was written well before anyone had ever heard of Anita Hill," says Deborah Pratt. "I felt it was important to show what women go through in the work place. I know what I have gone through as a woman in Hollywood. In one scene in the show, Scott is in the restaurant, and the boss places his hand on Scott's knee. Scott didn't react in the way I felt he should have. I thought he should have been outraged. Scott told me that, as a man, he didn't feel threatened by this gesture. After all, Sam's character could deck him."

During the shoot, miniskirted Scott complained of too many drafts and of being cold. He doesn't know how women do it.

Original airdate: October 25, 1989

"THE LEAP BETWEEN THE STATES,"
SEPTEMBER 20, 1962
Written by Richard C. Okie
Directed by David Hemmings

SHOULD BE:
SEPT 20, 1862

Sam leaps into a wounded Captain Beckett holding a dying comrade in his arms. Isaac finds Sam/Capt. Beckett and takes him back to his barn to nurse him to health. Al tells Sam he's in 1862 Virginia, and Sam realizes he is his own great grandfather. Olivia, a Southern belle, has Isaac put Sam in shackles, because in the past the Yankee army had ransacked her home. As Olivia is cleaning Sam's wound, she tells him how Yankees killed her husband and her herd, and tore up her property. She warns Sam the Virginia Patrol is coming for him. Al tells Sam his great-grandmother's name was Olivia Covington. Olivia's barn catches fire, and she unshackles Sam so he can help put out the blaze.

Three confederate soldiers approach Olivia's house. Lieutenant Montgomery looks at Sam in a puzzled way as he introduces himself as Olivia's cousin, hoping she won't turn him in. The soldiers are searching for runaway slaves. Sam walks into the barn and bumps into a black family, and as he approaches them, Isaac sticks a gun in Sam's face. Sam tries to help the slaves Isaac has sheltered, but Montgomery and his men show up at the barn and take Isaac away for harboring slaves. As Isaac and the slaves are about to be lynched, Sam orders Montgomery to wait until sunrise. He claims to be a Confederate captain, outranking Montgomery. His orders are honored. Sam slips brandy into Montgomery's after-dinner coffee. As Montgomery and Olivia are dancing to pass the time before sunrise, Sam brings the spiked coffee to two other soldiers. Montgomery makes several advances toward Olivia and admits he knows that Sam is a Yankee, because he found Sam's uniform rolled up in the shed. Sam enters the room with a gun, and Montgomery grabs Olivia to shield himself. he pulls his own gun and fires on Sam, who jumps at the reb lieutenant, pushing his hand into a kerosene lamp. Isaac decides to take on the name King once he becomes free. Al tells Sam that Isaac goes on to have a very famous grandson!

Original airdate: March 30, 1993

"NUCLEAR FAMILY," OCTOBER 26, 1962
Written by Paul Brown
Directed by James Whitmore, Jr.

In civil defense gear Sam is being told to put on his gas mask. The eerie hum of an emergency broadcast emanates from a portable radio. Sam hears the words, "Duck and cover!" He sees a mother with two small children wearing gas masks, protective goggles, and helmets. Someone yells something about "Rooskies," and "World War Three."

This is not a nightmare, but a salespitch for atom-bomb shelters. Sam is Eddie Elroy, a young man who is helping his brother sell paranoia and fear during the Cuban Missile Crisis.

Al tells Sam that the fear of a nuclear attack consumes this family. He must help the family relieve their panic and stop a member from accidentally shooting a neighbor, whom he saw as an invading Russian soldier.

Original airdate: May 15, 1991

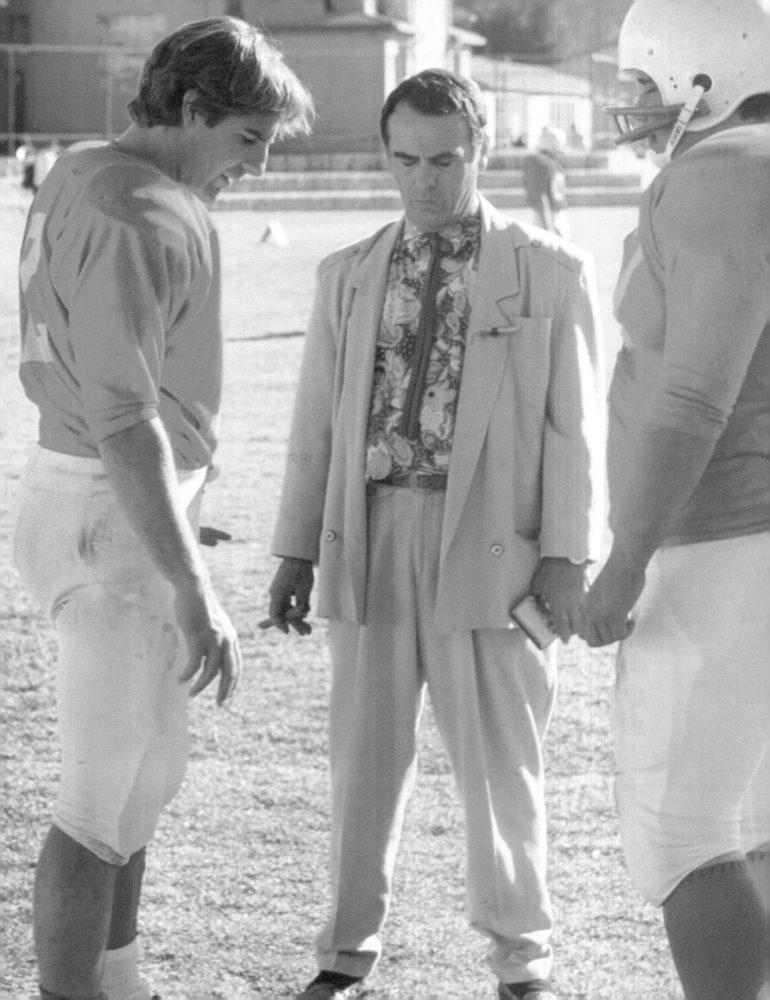

"ALL AMERICANS," NOVEMBER 6, 1962
Written by Paul Brown and Donald P. Bellisario
Directed by John Cullum

Sam receives a football pass and is tackled by teenage football players during a practice game. Sam is Eddie Vega, the quarterback for the Jaguars at El Camino High School in Southern California.

Sam has to help his Mexican-American teammate resist the pressure and stop him from forfeiting a game. If he succumbs to the pressure any hope he had for a promising future will be destroyed.

The episode director, John Cullum, plays Holling, owner of Cicely, Alaska's bar in *Northern Exposure*.

Original airdate: January 17, 1990

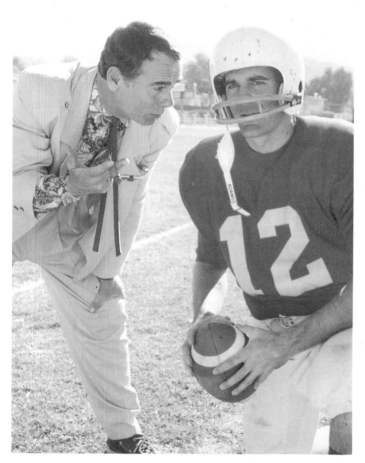

"A LITTLE MIRACLE," DECEMBER 24, 1962
Story by Sandy Fries
Teleplay by Sandy Fries and Robert A. Wolterstorff
Directed by Michael Watkins

Sam is in a crouching position holding out a pair of boxer shorts. A pair of hairy legs approach him. This man, whoever he is, expects Sam to dress him. In a mirror Sam sees a Santa Claus-type looking back at him.

He is Reginald Pearson, personal valet to real estate developer Michael G. Blake, the kind of man who put the word "raider" in "corporate raider."

In this twist on *A Christmas Carol,* Sam and Al must inject Blake with the spirit of Christmas to stop him from tearing down the mission.

In this episode Blake can actually see Al because of some chemical imbalance in the tycoon's brain. Al plays the ghost of Christmas Future with surprising results.

Original airdate: December 21, 1990

"MAYBE BABY," MARCH 11, 1963
Written by Paul Brown and Julie Brown
Directed by Michael Zinberg

Sam finds himself climbing down a ladder while a red-haired woman in a tacky Texas outfit holds it steady and tells him to hurry. They run toward a beat-up pickup truck. Inside the truck, a baby starts to cry. Sam has just been an accomplice in a kidnapping.

Sam is Buster, a bouncer at a strip joint in Waco, Texas, who is helping Bunny, a stripper, kidnap her baby. They head for New Mexico.

Al tells Sam that the baby is not really Bunny's. Sam must return the baby to her father, but Bunny is not about to let this happen.

This episode guest starred Julie Brown, the writer-singer-actress-comedian and sister of the show's producer Paul Brown.

Original airdate: April 4, 1990

"A SONG FOR THE SOUL," APRIL 7, 1963
Written by Deborah Pratt
Directed by Michael Watkins

Sam leaps into the body of Cheree, a member of the Lovettes singing group. He must stop Lynell, one of the trio, from leaving school to make it as a singer.

After performing at a Chicago nightclub, the trio—Lynell, Cheree, and Paula—is scolded by Lynell's father, Reverend Walters, for coming home at two A.M. Lynell reveals to Sam that her father allowed her late mother out of the house only to go to church, and that, she believes, is what killed her.

Al teaches Sam a few Temptations steps to perform at the club.

When Bobby Lee, a part-time pimp, turns up at Lynell's house, Sam/Cheree tells Lynell he'll convince her father to come watch them sing, but in return, if they get a record deal, she must finish school and not sign with Bobby Lee.

Before the tryout, Bobby Lee tries to rape Lynell, but Sam stops him. Reluctantly, Reverend Walters approves of his daughter's singing, and the Lovettes win the competition. Lynell also gains enough self-respect to tell Bobby Lee he has no record deal with her and to let her father know she has always respected his preachings.

Original airdate: February 26, 1992

"LEAP OF FAITH," AUGUST 19, 1963
Story by Nick Harding, Karen Hall, and Tommy Thompson
Teleplay by Tommy Thompson
Directed by James Whitmore, Jr.

Sam sees a young man dressed in a blue tuxedo staring at him, seemingly waiting for Sam to do something. Sam then sees a young lady in a wedding dress. She lifts her veil to see what is delaying her wedding.

It is Sam. He is Father Frank Pistano, a novice priest.

Sam is here to help another priest, guilt-ridden Father Mac, who is becoming an abusive drinker.

Al tells Sam that Father Mac will be murdered, because he has been witness to a robbery, but Sam soon realizes he must risk his own life by getting in the way of Father Mac's murder.

Al comes to terms with his own father's death in this episode. Sam must also help Father Mac from losing his faith to alcoholism.

Original airdate: October 12, 1990

"LEE HARVEY OSWALD," NOVEMBER 22, 1963
Written by Donald P. Bellisario
Directed by James Whitmore, Jr.

In Dallas, March 1963, Sam finds himself posing with a rifle as a woman named Marina takes his photo. To his amazement he speaks Russian to her, and she calls him Alik. Then in a leap lasting a brief moment, in the crosshairs of the rifle he is holding, he sights President Kennedy. In the instant he presses the trigger, he leaps backward to Atsugi, Japan, 1957, on a firing range where his bullet hits a target dead center. For no reason he is uncontrollably rude to the NCO trainer, making an enemy of the man. So when Al tells Sam that he leaped into Lee Harvey Oswald, Sam realizes he has Oswald's harsh personality. He also discovers he can do Oswald's job as a radar operator.

Later, in a bar where Sam/Oswald meets a prostitute who is teaching him Russian, Lopez, his sergeant, baits him, and during the ensuing brawl Oswald's personality takes over completely. He is about to shoot Lopez point blank in the head when Al desperately pulls Sam's consciousness back by quizzing him on quantum physics. Al explains to Sam that Lopez, who was originally killed by Oswald, will now live to save seventeen marines in battle.

After a brief leap to 1959 in Tustin, California, Sam leaps to KGB headquarters in Moscow where, as Oswald, he is relating military secrets he acquired during his time in the U.S. Marine Corps. At the same time, the real Oswald, in the Imaging Chamber, discovers to his amazement that he looks like Sam and is repeating scientific information from Sam's mind. Al interrupts Sam/Oswald in Moscow, forces Sam to regain his mind, and tells him that he must follow history for the moment and attempt suicide as Oswald did. The act prolonged Oswald's stay in the USSR where he met Marina. As Sam/Oswald cuts into his wrist with a razor, he leaps to Dallas, April 10, 1963. As Oswald, he has just tried to shoot General Walker, a right-wing army officer. Ziggy calculates the leaps back and forth are an attempt to unite Sam and Oswald's minds and reconnect them using DNA typing, but the process is complicating the situation further.

Sam/Oswald leaps to Dallas, Texas. It is November 22, 1963. He watches John F. Kennedy on television, then removes his wedding ring and leaves with his Mannlicher-Carcano rifle. As the presidential motorcade begins, Al, in the Imaging Chamber, forces Oswald to admit that, under his alias of Alik J. Hidell, he is going to shoot the President, and that he is acting alone.

On the sixth floor of the Dallas Book Depository, Sam/Oswald gets Kennedy in his sights, but as he pulls the trigger, Sam leaps into the Secret Service agent close to the presidential car, protecting Jackie Kennedy as her husband is being shot and saving her life. Al explains to Sam that in the first attempt, Oswald assassinated the President and the First Lady. On Sam's reaction, the familiar blue light envelops him and he leaps.

Original airdate: September 22, 1992

"BLIND FAITH," FEBRUARY 6, 1964
Written by Scott Shepherd
Directed by David Phinney

Sam finds himself center stage at New York's Carnegie Hall, sporting sunglasses, hands resting on a piano keyboard. He looks out at the audience and five thousand eyes stare back. He doesn't know what to do.

The audience gives a wild standing ovation. Sam stands, bows, and starts to walk offstage. He hears a bark, turns, and finds he has left his dog Chopin on stage!

Sam is blind. The dog starts to growl, sensing that Sam is not his real master. Michele Stevens, Sam's assistant, a mousy, twentyish girl, calls the dog off the stage. Sam has Quantum Leaped into Andrew Ross, a concert pianist.

Sam reads in the paper about a man who is murdering women in Central Park. He learns that, following his concert, Michele will be the next victim.

Original airdate: November 1, 1989

"RUNNING FOR HONOR," JUNE 11, 1964
Written by Bobby Duncan
Directed by Bob Hulme

Sam leaps into Cadet Commander Tommy York, a brilliant student at Prescott Naval Academy and a star sprinter. He must save Tommy's career and the life of Phillip Ashcroft, Tommy's ex-roommate, who has been run out of the Academy by a gang of gay-bashing cadets.

After learning about the homophobic cadets, Sam/Tommy goes to meet Phillip at a warehouse, where he is printing an underground newspaper. Ignoring Al's warning not to go, he finds Phillip being beaten by the bashers, who turn on Sam and report him to the admiral.

Confined to his room until after the track meet, Sam defends himself against Al, who agrees with the military attitudes toward homosexuals and teases Sam/Tommy. Al reports that Tommy heads a list of gay cadets that Phillip intends to publish, and that this list will be found on Phillip's body after he's found hanged in the warehouse.

The coach offers to help, and together they confront the gang, challenging its leader's sexuality and forcing him to confront his conflicted feelings. But, according to Ziggy, Phillip will still die.

At the warehouse, Sam and the coach find Phillip just before he's to stage his own hanging, and the coach reveals that he, too, is gay.

The next day, at the track meet, Al admits he's changed his own attitudes toward gays. Phillip, in the stands, gives a thumbs-up, and Al reveals that Phillip will go on to found the Gay Liberation Movement.

This is the most controversial episode *Quantum Leap* has yet aired. When it was in production, threatened advertiser defections caused a storm of charges and countercharges in Hollywood. Amidst threats of boycott and charges of censorship, the episode aired, essentially as written, to high ratings.

Original airdate: January 15, 1992

SHOULD BE:
July 4, 1964

"RUNAWAY," JULY 3, 1964
Written by Paul Brown
Directed by Michael Katelman

Sam leaps into the body of thirteen-year-old Butchie Rickett, who must keep his mother from running out on her family.

Butchie lives with his father, Hank, an ex-high school football player; his mother, Emma, a former high school valedictorian; and his older tomboy sister, Alex.

The family has embarked on a cross-country trip, and Sam/Butchie has to keep Emma, who is frustrated because she married rather than continuing her education, from disappearing forever. If she does, Alex will get pregnant and Butchie will never finish high school.

When she does run off after an argument with her husband, Al tells Sam that Emma's skeletal remains were discovered at the base of a nearby ridge.

Sam/Butchie and Hank arrive just in time to save her, and, Al later tells Sam, Emma goes off to college and becomes a teacher at the university. She and Hank live happily ever after.

Original airdate: January 5, 1991

"JIMMY," OCTOBER 14, 1964
Written by Paul M. Belous and Robert Wolterstorff
Directed by James Whitmore, Jr.

Sam finds himself sitting on the bottom of a bunk bed dressed in a Bullwinkle T-shirt and boxer shorts, and takes delight in the thought that he is a kid.

He looks at who he assumes to be his eight-year-old brother, Cory, shooting at him with a toy ray gun. Frank La Matta walks in and loses his patience with Sam, because he is not dressed yet and he will be late for his interview.

Sam sees himself in the mirror for the first time. He is not a boy, but a mentally retarded adult.

Frank is his brother, who is attempting to help Sam by getting him a job on the docks. Prejudice is everywhere.

Al tells Sam that if he doesn't stop the bullies on the docks from getting him fired, the man will die in a state home.

This is a special episode for Al. When he and his sister were orphaned, she was committed and didn't survive; Al never had the chance to save her and he desperately wants to help Jimmy. This episode also dealt with illiteracy.

Original airdate: November 22, 1989

"THE BOOGIEMAN," OCTOBER 31, 1964
Written by Chris Ruppenthal
Directed by Joe Napolitano

A lit candle, a book on witchcraft, a Victorian parlor: It's all too quiet and all too much like a "B" horror movie. Suddenly, a giant bug appears that sends Sam screaming and then the Devil turns up.

This Halloween show features Dean Stockwell's dual role as Al and the Devil.

Sam has to prevent the Devil from murdering his "girlfriend" and research assistant. Sam also happens to meet a young Stephen King and gives him ideas for his next few novels.

Original airdate: October 26, 1990

"JUSTICE," MAY 11, 1965
Written by Tony Graphia
Directed by Rob Bowman

Sam finds himself in the middle of a circle of men in Ku Klux Klan hoods and robes. He's Clyde, who works in the county voter registration office, and he's being inducted into the Klan.

Gene, the Grand Dragon and father of Clyde's wife, Lilly, is delighted that his son-in-law has joined.

At home, as Clyde and Lilly are being served by Ada, their black housekeeper, seven-year-old Cody appears holding a rifle.

When Sam/Clyde takes the gun away, the boy explains that he's just protecting himself against blacks—as his grandfather taught him. Much to Ada's and Lilly's surprise, Clyde demands Cody apologize to the black woman.

In the morning Clyde and Tom, a coworker, arrive at work to find two black men, Ada's son Nathaniel and a friend, waiting to register to vote.

After they're turned away by Tom, Clyde pleads with Ada to convince her son not to take on the entire town alone. Gene rushes in and tells Clyde that tonight the KKK will grab Nathaniel; Clyde stops Nathaniel from marching into the trap.

Gene and Tom tie up Clyde, while they go to blow up a black church. Cody overhears their conversation and frees Sam/Clyde, while Al appears to the children inside the church and convinces them to flee.

Clyde and Nathaniel arrive just as the church explodes. The Klansmen grab Nathaniel and put a noose around his neck. The federal marshalls, called by Lilly, arrive just in time.

The next day Lilly, Nathaniel, and Ada go to the courthouse to register to vote.

Original airdate: October 9, 1991

"ONE STROBE OVER THE LINE," JUNE 15, 1965
Written by Chris Ruppenthal
Directed by Michael Zinberg

A huge lion snarls at Sam. Just as it lunges toward him, Edie Landsdale, a gorgeous model wearing a stunning gown, pulls on the lion's leash.

Sam is Karl Granson, a top fashion photographer, who is having an exceptional day.

Al pops in to inform Sam that Edie is the only top model in an agency that is near bankruptcy. The agency people are loading her up with pep pills to keep her going during work hours. They don't mix well with the alcohol she consumes to put herself to sleep at night.

If Sam doesn't assist her within thirty-seven hours, she will be dead.

Original airdate: October 19, 1990

91

"BLACK ON WHITE ON FIRE,"
AUGUST 11, 1965
Written by Deborah Pratt
Directed by Joe Napolitano

Sam finds himself in a nice position, kissing a pretty blond. Suddenly, several black men are rushing toward Sam, and they don't look happy.

Sam is Ray Jordan, a black medical student in love with a white girl. Their love affair is not approved of by either community, black or white. They are a racial Romeo and Juliet.

Sam has to try to keep their relationship together during the violence of the Watts riots in Los Angeles. If he fails, Ray will lose his desire to become a doctor. The show used stock footage from the Watts riots.

Original airdate: November 9, 1990

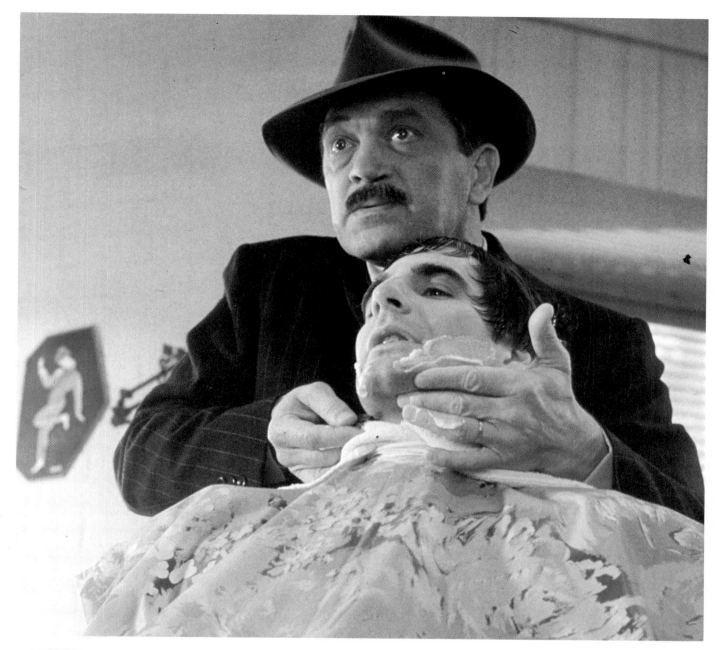

"DOUBLE IDENTITY," NOVEMBER 8, 1965
Written by Donald P. Bellisario
Directed by Aaron Lipstadt

Sam is in an attic with a beautiful Italian woman. They have just finished making love. She tells him he was terrific.

Sam is Frankie La Palma, an Italian romeo and a mob hit man, who is having an affair with the wrong woman, or rather, the wrong man's woman.

Set in South Brooklyn, the story involves an elaborate Italian wedding, a team of comical thugs, and Scott singing "Volare."

Sam has to convince a hit man to leave the mob and also causes the Blackout of 1965 by simply plugging in a hair dryer.

Original airdate: April 21, 1989

"DELIVER US FROM EVIL,"
MARCH 19, 1966
Written by Robin Jill Bernheim, Deborah Pratt, and Tommy Thompson
Directed by Bob Hume

Frank tells his wife Connie that he and Sam/Jimmy have to run errands, but actually they are helping Frank's girlfriend Shirley move into a new apartment. Al appears to inform Sam that Connie is set to have Jimmy institutionalized because he is retarded. Al also recalls that his own sister was in an orphanage; when she came down with pneumonia, she was moved to a mental hospital, and he never saw her again. Sam must make sure that Jimmy does not meet with the same fate.

Trying to help Frank and Connie save their marriage, Sam/Jimmy is telling Connie how much Frank needs her, but she says Frank is jealous of him. Their conversation gets very emotional, and Sam/Jimmy grabs Connie by her shoulders. A quantum circuit connects, and Connie becomes another person, dangerously beautiful, with fire in her eyes. She is transformed into Alia, the time traveler, and there is an immediate connection between Sam and Alia.

Connie/Alia lures Sam/Jimmy into the bedroom, and when Frank catches them together, Connie tells Frank that Jimmy tried to rape her. She urges Frank to call his doctor to commit him. Alia's partner Zoey tells her that she must kill Sam/Jimmy, and Al reads the next day's newspaper headlines, which indicate that Connie is being arraigned for killing Jimmy in self-defense. In a confrontation between Connie/Alia and Sam/Jimmy, Alia points a gun at Jimmy, who grabs and fires it. A swell of energy engulfs Alia and Zoey as they disappear. The following day, there is no mention in the papers of any violence. Sam and Al exchange a look, a bright light engulfs Sam and Al, and they leap.

Original airdate: November 10, 1992

"STAR LIGHT, STAR BRIGHT,"
MAY 21, 1966
Written by Richard C. Okie
Directed by Chris Hibler

Sam/Max disappears into the woods with his grandson, Tim Stoddard, in search of a UFO. They are found by John, Tim's father and Max's son, who feels his dad is losing his mind. A little later John and his wife Eva spot Sam/Max in his bedroom talking to Al, whom they cannot see, and think he is talking to himself. They decide he would be better off in a mental institution, which prompts Sam to ask Al to look up the town's history of UFO sightings. Meanwhile, the government has sent Dr. Burton Hardy and Major Meadows to keep a close eye on Sam/Max. They believe there have been UFO sightings, and Sam/Max may have valuable information.

Tim tells Sam/Max that he is running away because he is being forced to go to school, when what he really wants to do is simply play his guitar. Sam/Max convinces Tim to go to school during the day and play his guitar at night. Later that night, Hardy and Meadows arrive at the Stoddard home to question Sam/Max about UFOs, but Al cautions him not to talk to them. Before leaving, they tell John Stoddard they will come back the next day, although their intentions are to get Sam/Max institutionalized so they can sedate and question him. To prepare Sam/Max, Al gives him UFO information, and Sam sees a definite pattern and knows there will be another sighting soon.

Sam/Max believes he is meeting Hardy and Meadows at their office, until he sees the state hospital sign. He fights to get away, but he is grabbed and strapped to the table where the doctor gives him sodium pentothal to make him talk. While under sedation, Sam begins to reveal Project Quantum Leap, but John and Tim storm into the room and snatch him away. As quickly as they can, the three run to where Sam/Max saw the UFO, and just as Hardy and Meadows grab Sam/Max, a burst of light fills the air and Sam is swept away.

Original airdate: October 27, 1992

"FOR YOUR LOVE," JUNE 14, 1966
(Part two of a trilogy beginning with "One Little Heart")
Written by Deborah Pratt
Directed by James Whitmore, Jr.

Sam/Will and Abagail are passionately in love and can hardly wait to wed, and bed, the next day. Sam realizes he has jumped from Abagail's father to potential husband, and soon understands why. Having saved her from the fire eleven years earlier, he must once more protect her from Leta and the narrow minds of the townsfolk.

Last night, Abagail was baby-sitting Pervis, the young son of Mrs. Takins. Today, she is preparing herself for her wedding, when the news spreads that Pervis cannot be found, and she was the last person to see him. He was upset that she was getting married and was sulking in his room when Takins paid her and she left their house. The wedding is postponed until the boy is found. That night, unable to spend any more time apart, Sam/Will and Abagail make love. Meanwhile, the townsfolk search the backwoods. Leta Aider is among them, threatening that she will see Abagail executed this time, and reminding everyone of her husband's and her daughter's death.

Only Al knows where Pervis will be found tomorrow morning, so Abagail must be kept safe until then. A man possessed, Sam/Will rushes back to Abagail at her house, and they spend the rest of the night making love. But in the early morning the townsfolk, led by Leta, take Abagail to be lynched, and Sam fights the frenzied townspeople until the crisis is over, and Leta is thwarted. The couple kiss deeply as Sam is washed in a flash of light, and he leaps.

Original airdate: November 24, 1992

"NOWHERE TO RUN," AUGUST 10, 1968
Written by Tommy Thompson
Directed by Alan Levi

Sam Beckett becomes Ron Miller, a legless Vietnam vet undergoing therapy at San Diego Veteran's Hospital in 1968. He is befriended by Kiki Wilson, a young volunteer nurse trying to keep herself busy while she waits for the return of her young brother, missing in action. He and Al witness Billy Johnson, a young black soldier crippled from the neck down, reject his girlfriend and send her away heartbroken. Al thinks that Billy is getting ready to kill himself because in two days he will be found at the bottom of the therapy pool.

Sam/Ron is visited by an uneasy Julie Miller, Ron's wife. Despite the discomfort between the couple, Al tells Sam to help make the marriage work because Ron later has three sons and the eldest will save the lives of his entire tank crew in the Gulf War. Sam/Ron takes Julie to a coffee house, and Al stays in the hospital to watch Billy Johnson. Thinking to cheer Billy up, Nurse Kiki provides him with an electric-powered wheelchair, in which he struggles to the therapy pool, determined to drown himself. Meanwhile at the coffee bar, Julie tells Sam/Ron that there is another man in her life, and she wants a divorce, just as a very concerned Al pops in to get Sam/Ron back to the hospital. There, Al becomes more frantic because an unsuspecting nurse lets Billy into the therapy pool.

Delayed by Julie's bad news, Sam/Ron is struggling to get to the pool when he is stopped and dragged back to his room by Holt, an unsympathetic and brutal orderly, ignoring the warning that Billy is about to kill himself. Realizing that something drastic must be done, Sam stands up, since he has legs even though Ron does not, and knocks out Holt. Back in the chair, Sam/Ron rushes to the therapy pool, where he stands up again to dive into the pool to retrieve Billy. Holt babbles on that Sam/Ron floated up from his wheelchair and knocked him out. It is assumed that Holt has lost his mind, and he is fired, although the staff cannot understand how a legless man could jump into the pool to save Billy.

After all these unusual events, Sam assumes that Ron will never have the son who saves his men, when Al realizes that Kiki is the woman for Ron. When Kiki is called to the hospital, she is carrying a telegram telling her that her brother is on his way home. Sam's mission is accomplished and the familiar blue light engulfs him.

Original airdate: October 6, 1992

"LIBERATION," OCTOBER 16, 1968
Written by Chris Abbot and Deborah Pratt
Directed by Bob Hulme

Sam leaps into the body of a sixties homemaker named Margaret. Sam/Margaret and daughter Suzi are arrested at a women's liberation rally at the university. Margaret's husband George immediately gets them out of jail because police chief Tipton's son is his employee. Sam/Margaret and Suzi argue with George with equal work deserves equal pay for men and women. Al tells Sam that there is another protest planned where the chief accidentally shoots Suzi's friend Diana St. Cloud when they struggle over a gun. Sam/Margaret interrupts the sit-in and tries to convince the women that they should fight for equal rights in the boardrooms, not in the streets.

Al tells Sam that the sequence has changed and that Suzi and Chief Tipton get shot when Suzi steps in front of Diana to save her. Women's libber Diana and her group take over the men's club. She is verbally abusive and yells about women being exploited as sex objects and domestic servants. Chief Tipton tries to remove Diana from the sit-in, but she pulls a gun on him. Sam/Margaret tries to talk her out of using it, but Diana waves the gun and tells her friend's mother she's been brainwashed to be a housewife. Suzi grabs the gun from Diana. It goes off. Sam/Margaret knocks Tipton to the ground as the bullet hits where he would have been standing. Al urges Sam/Margaret that she must save the marriage because George is getting ready to leave her. Sam/Margaret tells George to go ahead and leave, unless he can understand that she's a person and has feelings and opinions. Just as they're about to kiss and make up, Sam leaps.

Original airdate: January 12, 1993

SHOULD BE:
October 19, 1967

"ANIMAL FRAT," OCTOBER 19, 1968
Written by Chris Ruppenthal
Directed by Gilbert Shilton

Sam finds himself lying on his back in the middle of a pool table surrounded by a crowd of chanting fraternity brothers and sorority sisters. A keg is above his head and beer is gushing down toward his open mouth. The chanters scream with excitement.

Sam is Knut Wileton, the John Belushi of Tau Kappa Beta.

Sam must stop Elizabeth Spokane, a serious student and antiwar protester, from bombing the university chemistry lab as a statement against the Vietnam War.

Original airdate: January 3, 1990

"MIA," APRIL 1, 1969
Written by Donald P. Bellisario
Directed by Michael Zinberg

Sam is wearing a miniskirt, a well-filled sweater, and red spike heels. He immediately assumes he is a hooker.

But then he hears voices coming over a radio. An antenna is sticking out of his purse.

Suddenly, there is chaos: hippie drug dealers, undercover cops, sawed-off shotguns. Weapons are pointing right at Sam. He hears a very unpleasant word: NARC!

Al tells Sam that he has to prevent a young woman from marrying, although her husband is missing in action and presumed dead.

The missing husband is Al, and she was his first love. Sam also has to stop a detective from being murdered by drug dealers.

Original airdate: May 9, 1990

"HURRICANE," AUGUST 17, 1969
Written by Chris Ruppenthal
Directed by Michael Watkins

Sam becomes Deputy Sheriff Archie Necaise. He finds himself in Jackson Point, Mississippi, with nurse/girlfriend Cissy Davis.

Hurricane Camille is about to hit with deadly force. Archie and Cissy are trying to convince the local residents to flee the storm, but the locals are having a hurricane party and refuse to leave.

Sam learns he must return to the party and evacuate the tenants or they will be killed. He also must prevent Cissy from returning to her own house, where she, too, will die. Complications arise when Cissy's ex-boyfriend shows up with his family, but Sam saves the tenants and Cissy.

After the hurricane passes, Sam encourages Cissy to become a psychotherapist.

Original airdate: October 2, 1991

"THE PLAY'S THE THING,"
SEPTEMBER 9, 1969
Story by Bobby Duncan and Beverly Bridges
Teleplay by Beverly Bridges
Directed by Eric Laneuville

Sam becomes New York actor Joe Thurlow, twenty-five, living with Jane Lindhurst, who is a day from her fiftieth birthday. When Jane's son and his pregnant wife arrive to take her home, Sam must persuade her to follow her dream of becoming a singer, and must also go on stage as Hamlet to save Joe's acting career.

Al tells him that in two days Jane will return to Cleveland and live out her life alone, but Ziggy has concluded that Sam is here to save Joe's life, not Jane's.

Joe never went on stage, blew his big break and became a real-estate salesman.

Two minutes to curtain, Sam discovers he must play the role in the nude, while Jane agrees to go back to Cleveland.

Sam goes on and an agent offers to sign him to be the new "Boxer Boy" in a series of underwear commercials. He agrees with one condition: the agent must audition a new singer for the commercial's jingle.

Sam sprints to Jane's apartment in time to convince her to do the audition. The agent, impressed, signs them both. Al reports that Joe and Jane got married and lived happily ever after.

Original airdate: January 8, 1992

"THE LEAP HOME, PART I,"
NOVEMBER 25, 1969
Written by Donald P. Bellisario
Directed by Joe Napolitano

Sam appears in a cornfield and seeing a farmhouse, he runs toward it, ignoring the gate and jumping the fence.

The window on the front porch has been turned into a mirror by the setting sun. Sam is home in Indiana, and can change the family's past.

He can get his father to stop smoking cigarettes and cut back on coffee. Then he will not die in five years. He can warn his brother, Tom, who is home from the navy for Thanksgiving, so that he won't die in Vietnam. He can help restore his sister's self-esteem, so she won't marry an alcoholic. He can change it all.

He could, if it were a perfect world. Al tells him he is here to win the basketball game that he lost in 1969. It will change many people's lives.

Scott also played his own father in this first part of a two-part *Quantum Leap.*

Michael Watkins, the director of photography, won his second consecutive Emmy for this two-part episode.

Original airdate: September 28, 1990

"VIETNAM—THE LEAP HOME, PART II,"
APRIL 7, 1970
Written by Donald P. Bellisario
Directed by Michael Zinberg

As Sam reaches out for his brother, Tom ("The Leap Home"), he finds himself with other soldiers in muddy water.

As his body rises from the water, so does his PRC-77 radio and a Stoner 63-A light machine gun, both of which are strapped on his back.

Sam is Herbert (Magic) Williams, a black Navy Seal on a mission in Vietnam.

Sam is amazed to find himself with his brother Tom. He arrives in time to save him, one day before Tom was killed.

Standing in Sam's way is the fact that the POW mission they are on, must be successful.

Co-Executive Producer Michael Zinberg won the Directors Guild Award for this episode.

Original airdate: October 5, 1990

"FREEDOM," NOVEMBER 22, 1970
Written by Chris Ruppenthal
Directed by Alan Levi

Sam leaps into George Washakie, a young American Shoshone Indian, being beaten by Sheriff Taggart, who is forty-six and mean as hell.

Sam is dragged to a jail cell and thrown in with an old Indian, Joseph Washakie, his grandfather. They have been arrested for "borrowing" a broken-down pickup truck. Sam escapes with Joseph, but they are on the run.

Sam can tell that Joseph is ill with emphysema. He wants to get him to a hospital. But Joseph assures Sam that he has oxygen at home. He wants to go to his own home, not back to the nursing home. So Sam now knows that he is here to save Joseph's life. But Al tells Sam he is here to help the grandfather die where he was born.

Sam can't do this, because Joseph needs medical attention, and he's a doctor. Al tells him that before Joseph dies, Sam must take him to the Indian reservation where he will be safe. If Sam doesn't, both will spend the next decade in jail.

Original airdate: February 14, 1990

"A PORTRAIT FOR TROIAN,"
FEBRUARY 7, 1971
Written by Scott Shepherd and Donald P. Bellisario
Directed by Michael Zinberg

Sam finds himself in a cemetery. The wind whistles, a dog is howling.

He sees Troian, a beautiful woman with long dark hair and blazing eyes, in search of something.

She rushes into a mausoleum, dragging Sam with her, repeating the name Julian.

He finds the tomb of Julian Claridge, dead since 1968. Electronic equipment is everywhere, and Troian thinks it has recorded Julian's voice print. Sam is Dr. Timothy Mintz, a ghost buster. Troian was a successful illustrator for the Gothic romances her husband Julian had written, until he drowned in the lake three years ago.

At a mansion, Troian's family worries that she is going crazy. This is the backdrop for a haunting mystery.

Al tells Sam that everyone in the Claridge family has died violent and unnatural deaths. Sam refuses to believe any of this, and has to figure out who is trying to drive Troian crazy.

Co-executive producer Deborah Pratt played Troian, which is also the name of her and Donald P. Bellisario's daughter. In the reflection in the mirror, which occurs in every show, Bellisario stared back at Sam. Truly a family affair. SHOULD BE:
        December 13, 1989
Original airdate: December 13, 1990

"BEFORE AN EXECUTION," MAY 12, 1971
Story by Bill Bigelow, Donald P. Bellisario, and Deborah Pratt
Teleplay by Deborah Pratt
Directed by Michael Watkins

Quantum Leaping occasionally can be difficult, but this leap could literally fry Sam.

Sam sits in an electric chair contemplating his last moments. He is Jesus Ortega, a murderer who has been condemned to die by the state of Florida.

Sam's character is guilty of the crime, but he must find a way to exonerate his innocent partner, who is also on death row.

Original airdate: May 1, 1991

LAST DANCE BEFORE
THE EXECUTION

"PROMISED LAND," DECEMBER 22, 1971
Written by Gillian Horvath and Tommy Thompson
Directed by Scott Bakula

It is Christmas and the Walters' farm, like most others around Elk Ridge, Indiana, is about to go under. Sam, as Bill Walters, finds himself in the middle of a holdup at the bank, along with elder brother Neil and younger brother John. Neil, having made the investment, plans to rob the bank of the exact amount owed, but it doesn't have enough money on hand. Soon a crowd, headed by Sheriff Mundy, has gathered outside.

Al reports that banker Gus Vernon, having already made a deal with a developer to build a massive shopping center on the farmland, manipulated the struggling farmers into investing in unnecessary equipment, then foreclosed when they couldn't pay back the loans. Sam remembers the hardships of his own family's attempt to work their farm, and reckons if he can find Vernon's development agreement, he can help all the farmers. Using a sympathetic pregnant teller as a diversion, he escapes from the surrounded bank, runs to Vernon's house, and finds the document. Vernon arrives, but is knocked out by Sam/Bill, who takes the agreement, and the banker, back to town.

Unfortunately, John Walters has been seriously wounded. Sheriff Mundy allows Sam/Bill to go back into the bank, calm down Neil, and get John to a hospital. Al reports that John recovers, while Neil does five years for assault then is killed in a robbery. Saddened, Sam leaves the bank, sees his own father, John Beckett, across the street and talks to him. As he hugs his confused father, a bright light engulfs Sam.

Original airdate: December 15, 1992

"STAR-CROSSED," JUNE 15, 1972
Written by Deborah Pratt
Directed by Mark Sobel

Sam leaps into a classroom at Lawrence College in Marion, Ohio.

He is Gerald Bryant, an English professor, who has two problems: young women and booze.

One overly romantic young woman, Jamie Lee, in particular, can't be quiet about her romance with Bryant. She has already informed Oscar, her Neanderthal boyfriend, and her father about her undying love for this man who is twice her age.

Al tells Sam that there will be a shotgun wedding in five days, and he must stop Jamie Lee from making the biggest mistake of her life.

To complicate matters, Sam has seen the only woman he thinks he has ever loved. She is Donna Eleese, Sam's ex-fiancée. He believes he's been given a second chance at love.

When Sam met Donna, they both felt they had known each other all their lives. They were to be married, but for some unknown reason, Donna never showed up at the chapel.

Al warns Sam that the first rule of the Quantum Leap project is not to change his future, but only the future of those around him.

Sam approaches Donna, who is a waitress, and tells her to look into his eyes. She thinks he is trying to hit on her, but stares into his eyes and knows exactly what he wants to order. This disturbs her and she leaves.

Oscar comes looking for Sam to "rearrange" his face, but Sam stops him by advising him to be more romantic with Jamie Lee. At home, Jamie Lee comes back for more, but Sam persuades her to give Oscar one more chance.

Al tells Sam he must leave Donna alone or he (Al) will be pulled off the project. Sam knows that he and Donna are star-crossed lovers.

Donna's father left her when she was eight, and she has not trusted men since. Sam was the second man she left at the altar. If Sam can get Donna and her father together, maybe he will change history. Maybe he will finally marry the woman he loved.

Original airdate: March 31, 1989

"THE BEAST WITHIN," NOVEMBER 6, 1972
Written by John D'Aquino
Directed by Gus Trikonis

Sam finds himself climbing out of a doctor's office window, when he is caught by Daniel Burke, a terribly frightened thirteen-year-old boy. Sam has leaped into the body of Henry Akers, a homeless Vietnam veteran, who has broken in to get medication for his sick buddy, Roy Brown. Karen and Luke, Daniel's mother and stepfather, come to the boy's rescue after hearing his screams for help. Daniel has mistaken Sam/Henry for Bigfoot and Luke tries to dispel Daniel's fears by leaving the find the intruder. Sam/Henry, a beastly looking man, returns to the woods, where he and Roy live. Daniel runs away to find the beast.

Reading Henry's journal, Sam learns that Luke married Karen, his best friend John Burke's wife, after Burke's death in Vietnam. Henry was ordered by Burke, his commanding officer, to secure an enemy hutch. Luke refused the order, so Burke went in himself and was killed by an explosion. There were only two witnesses to the disobeyed orders—Henry and Roy. They never came forward. All four of the young men were high school friends. Sam is interrupted by Roy having a seizure, caused by a wartime head wound. Seeing Roy's condition worsening, Sam, thinking quickly, remembers that the local wild Lobelia flower contains a natural relaxant that will help Roy until medicine is available.

Daniel reaches Sam/Henry and Roy's camp, hungry and scared. Sam/Henry and Roy try to calm the boy by relating a similar story about seeing Bigfoot at Williamette Peak, just as Daniel had with his father. At this point, Roy's condition takes a turn for the worse. Sam has no choice but to head back to town for medicine, leaving Daniel to care for Roy. Luke and his deputy are preparing to set out for Daniel and the two fugitives, when Sam/Henry confronts him with Roy's illness and the need for immediate medical care, but Deputy Curtis, rifle in hand, arrests Sam/Henry. Roy and Daniel decide to make their way to Williamette Peak to prove Luke wrong by finding and photographing the beast. Al finds Sam/Henry in jail and warns him about Roy and Daniel's ill fate should he not reach them. Daniel's mom, Karen, enters looking for Luke. With the little information that he has, Sam convinces Karen to take him to the peak.

Roy and Daniel settle in, waiting for the perfect shot, when Daniel's camera falls off the edge with the boy following and landing in a crevice. Roy panics. Al tells Sam/Henry of the trouble with Daniel. Just then, Karen's truck tips over into a ditch, forcing them to the peak on foot. They reach Roy, who can only say, "Daniel fell." Al relays to Sam the information on the boy, as Luke arrives just in time to help. They all team together to get Daniel back to safety. The crevice is only wide enough for a small body, which leaves only Roy to save the boy. Although apprehensive, he sets aside his fears to rescue Daniel. When they reach the truck, they find it has been moved onto the road, ready to use. Sam gets Daniel inside, next to Karen and Luke. They offer to take Roy along to the hospital. Sam is on his way back to town on foot. Al says Karen and Luke go on to have two kids and Roy becomes a fire watcher with the Forestry Service. Henry turns his journal into a best-seller. Al and Sam turn to see what appears to be Bigfoot making his way back to the woods. Sam leaps.

Original airdate: March 16, 1993

"HER CHARM," SEPTEMBER 26, 1973
Story by Paul M. Belous, Robert Wolterstorff, Deborah Pratt, and Donald P. Bellisario
Teleplay by Deborah Pratt and Donald P. Bellisario
Directed by Chris Welch

Sam is standing at a door ringing the bell. A woman yells at him to stop. She will be right out. She stomps out of the house, complaining the entire way to the car parked in the front driveway. In the car, Sam doesn't know where he is supposed to be going.

A Mercedes stops at the end of the driveway and a burst of bullets is fired their way. Sam pulls her down on the seat next to him. Glass shatters everywhere, but Sam has saved the woman and himself. Still, she never stops complaining.

Sam is Peter Langly, a crooked FBI agent. His job is to protect Dana Barrenger until she testifies and can be put into the Federal Witness Protection Program. She never stops nagging and complaining. In her eyes, Sam can't do anything right.

Original airdate: February 7, 1990

SHOULD BE:
February 2, 1974

"THOU SHALT NOT..." FEBRUARY 3, 1974
Written by Tammy Ader
Directed by Randy Roberts

Finding himself in a Jewish Temple in Los Angeles, Sam stares down at a thirteen-year-old girl chanting in Hebrew the final prayer of her Bat Mitzvah ceremony.

As she finished she looks to Sam for guidance. A Cantor jumps in to save Sam from this uncomfortable silence. Sam sees his reflection in the gold-plated tabernacle. Sam looks and says, "Oy vey. I'm a rabbi."

Sam must prevent an affair the mother is about to have that will destroy the family that has never come to terms with the accidental death of their son.

While having dinner, Sam introduces the Heimlich maneuver, to, of all people, Dr. Heimlich.

Original airdate: November 15, 1989

117

"GLITTER ROCK," APRIL 12, 1974
Written by Chris Ruppenthal
Directed by Andy Cadiff

A rock performer stands center stage in a huge arena in Detroit. It is the middle of a roaring rock concert. His face is painted with a lightning bolt, his clothes are wildly colorful, and he's wearing platform shoes. Eighty-thousand screaming fans are loving Sam!

As the lead singer in a glitter rock band, Sam has to discover who murdered him in 1974. One of the suspects is an out-of-control fan who has been stalking the band, and claims to be the singer's son. Sam has to find out the truth in order to leap.

Original airdate: April 10, 1991

"THE GREAT SPONTINI," MAY 9, 1974
Written by Cristy Dawson and Beverly Bridges
Directed by James Whitmore, Jr.

Sam appears to be crammed into some sort of box. He hears two taps on the trunk and then a drum roll. A saber slices through the trunk, whisking right by his nose. Another saber slices past his shoulder, and a third just misses his groin. Sam is "The Great Spontini," a second-rate magician.

Not only must Sam battle for custody of his twelve-year-old daughter, but he must also stop the magician from killing her when a magic trick becomes dangerous.

Original airdate: November 16, 1990

"THE RIGHT HAND OF GOD,"
OCTOBER 24, 1974
Written by John Hill
Directed by Gilbert Shilton

Finding himself in a boxing ring, in the middle of a fight, Sam isn't sure how to respond to his rather large opponent.

He does what anyone who isn't a fighter would do; he takes a hard blow and staggers back into the ropes. The crowd begins to boo and yell as Sam attempts to protect his body from the other fighter. Sam finally decides to fight back. He throws a punch, and though it barely connects, his burly opponent takes it and falls down for the count. Sam is "Kid Cody," a winner!

Sam meets Sister Sarah, a nun who owns Kid's contract as part of an estate. It is no surprise to Sam that Kid's fights have been fixed.

Al informs Sam that he must win a fight fairly, so the nuns can use the prize money to build a chapel for the poor and destitute.

Original airdate: April 4, 1989

"BLOOD MOON," MARCH 10, 1975
Written by Tommy Thompson
Directed by Alan Levi

Al tells Sam he is one of London's most eccentric and expensive artists, and has leaped to prevent his wife Alexandria from being murdered and drained of her blood. Friends, Victor and Claudia, arrive at Sam/Nigel's castle for dinner and to watch the Blood Moon ritual. Victor presents Sam/Nigel and Alexandria with a silver dagger. Knowing it is a few hours before the Blood Moon, Claudia and Victor invite Sam/Nigel and Alexandria to join them in bed. Al tells Sam it's characteristic of vampires to engage in "group activities," and explains to him that Blood Moon is a sacred night that occurs once every ten years. It's the night the walking dead honor Count Bathory, one of the first vampires, who, walled up by the townspeople, lived for three years by drinking his own blood. The night he died the moon turned blood red. Al says that Alexandria is found dead, drained of blood. The murder weapon is a silver dagger.

Victor calls for a last toast before the ritual, and Sam/Nigel takes a sip of their drink, only to find it is drugged. Victor says the count now has two offerings. Claudia is ready to sink her teeth into Sam/Nigel's neck when Horst, the butler, knocks her over and unties him. Claudia and Sam/Nigel struggle and as she lies on the ground, he learns her fangs are fake. Sam/Nigel catches up with Victor who has Alexandria tied up on the roof, and shows Victor Claudia's phony fangs. Just as Victor is about to kill Alexandria with the dagger, it is struck by lightning. Victor is killed and Alexandria, realizing that Nigel is a vampire, becomes a missionary.

Original airdate: February 9, 1993

"DISCO INFERNO," APRIL 1, 1976
Written by Paul Brown
Directed by Gilbert Shilton

Sam finds himself in a white, three-piece polyester suit. He wears platform shoes and strikes a Travolta pose, while a pretty blond is spinning around him.

Suddenly thugs rush into the disco and blast Sam with a machine gun. A director yells, "Cut!"

Sam is Chad Stone, a stunt man in a "B" disco movie.

Chad's father is the show's stunt coordinator and responsible for hiring Chad. He looks out for his own boys. He has a younger brother, who also wants to go into the stunt business.

Al tells Sam that Chris will die attempting his first stunt.

Sam endeavors to stop Chris, who accuses him of trying to stand in his way and steal his girlfriend. All Chris wants is the respect he has never received from his father.

Sam remembers he had a real older brother, too. This memory provokes Sam to do all he can to save Chris.

Original airdate: September 27, 1989

"A HUNTING WE WILL GO," JUNE 18, 1976
Written by Beverly Bridges
Directed by Andy Cadiff

Standing in a phone booth, Sam is attempting to talk to someone. A woman starts calling out for help. Sam is handcuffed to this woman, who is yelling that he has kidnapped her. A couple of men come to her aid and work Sam over.

Sam is not a kidnapper, but is Gordon O'Reilly, a bounty hunter in the South. And the pretty blond, Diane Frost, is his bounty.

In a variation on *The Taming of the Shrew,* Diane is a real wildcat, accused of embezzling money from her boss.

Sam realizes that she, in fact, did not embezzle the money. Diane actually took the money to protect several elderly investors.

Original airdate: April 17, 1991

SHOULD BE:
February 28, 1979

"DREAMS," FEBRUARY 28, 1978
Written by Deborah Pratt
Directed by Anita Addison

Sam leaps into Lt. Jack Stone, who is investigating the murder of a woman in her Malibu home. Sam is affected by something horrible that happened to Jack, which he must overcome to catch the killer and save himself.

Sam and his partner, Pamela Rosseli, find the mutilated body of Janice Decaro. Her husband Peter is in another room, traumatized and with a gun in his hand. Their two terrified children are found in the shower.

Sam/Jack feels terror himself when he tries to open the bathroom door again. Sam believes part of Jack's personality has remained, and he demands information from a very concerned Al, who's had difficulty tracking Sam, because Sam's brainwaves are scrambled.

From Ziggy he learns that in two days Jack will be murdered in the Decaro house, which means Sam will die.

Sam and Pamela visit Decaro's psychiatrist, Mason Crane, and that night Sam breaks into his office.

At a meeting the next day with the psychiatrist, Al suddenly appears and urges Sam to leave immediately. Ziggy has found out that Jack and Janice had had an affair and that Jack is the killer. Sam doesn't believe it.

He returns to the Decaro house with the psychiatrist, who hypnotizes him. Sam realizes Jack's nightmare stems from witnessing his own mother's autopsy.

Crane admits that he is the murderer and urges the hypnotized Sam to shoot himself. But Sam is conscious and shoots Crane, thus saving Jack, who marries Pamela and retires to Florida.

Original airdate: November 13, 1991

"THE LAST DOOR," JULY 28, 1978
(Part three of a trilogy beginning
with "One Little Heart")
Written by Deborah Pratt
Directed by James Whitmore, Jr.

Marie finds Sam/Lawrence Stanton and solicits his help to prove Abagail innocent, and Al tells Sam that Abagail was sentenced to the electric chair. Al also informs him that Violet Aider's bones were found sealed in the well and that she was not killed by a pack of wild dogs.

Later, Abagail tells Sam/Lawrence that she found Aider with her throat slashed, but didn't call the police because she was in shock. Sheriff Bo Loman showed up at the scene, saying he got a call from someone who heard a woman screaming. When Sam/Lawrence realizes Abagail has a daughter, Al explains to Sam that Sammy Jo is his daughter.

Sam/Lawrence decides to go to the mental institution to seek answers from Laura Fuller. She remembered how Sam was supposed to marry her daughter years ago (part two). Laura gives Sam/Lawrence the locket that Violet and Abagail originally fought over and later tells the jury that she knocked Violet into the well and went to grab her, although all she came up with was the locket. Laura had informed her husband Clayton what had happened, and he immediately sealed the well and told the townspeople that Violet was eaten by a pack of wild dogs. The prosecutor for the state tries to discredit Laura by telling the jury she is institutionalized and not a reliable witness.

Sam/Lawrence decides to put Abagail on the stand because he found a piece of evidence. Abagail tells Sam/Lawrence that when she walked into the house and found Leta, the knife was beside Leta's body. Sam/Lawrence shows a phone bill that proves somebody called the sheriff's office twenty-two minutes before she walked into the house. Sam/Lawrence declares that Leta came to Abagail's house in a rage, called the sheriff, and slit her own throat with one of Abagail's knives. Suddenly, Sammy Jo emerges and tells the court she saw Leta kill herself. Later, Al reveals to Sam that Abagail gets married in two years and moves to Chicago. The familiar light engulfs Sam and he leaps.

Original airdate: November 24, 1992

"CATCH A FALLING STAR," MAY 21, 1979
Written by Paul Brown
Directed by Donald P. Bellisario

Sam sits in front of a mirror, while a woman applies makeup to his face to age him. Through the door he hears the overture to *Man of La Mancha*.

An obviously nervous stagehand runs in to tell Sam he has to be on in sixty seconds.

This is a nightmare: You must perform on stage in a play, but you don't know one single line! Just as Sam is about to have a breakdown, the lead walks on and starts to sing. John Cullum, who starred in *Man of La Mancha* in several national tours, guest stars here as the actor Sam must help.

In order to Quantum Leap, Sam has to prevent an aging actor from ruining his career.

This crosses Sam's real history as well. He has to come to terms with a teenage crush he had on his piano teacher.

Original airdate: December 6, 1989

"PRIVATE DANCER," OCTOBER 6, 1979
Written by Paul Brown
Directed by Debbie Allen

Wearing a skimpy version of a Zorro outfit, Sam hears the beat of sexy rock music. Women swoon, kiss and grope at his briefs which are overflowing with currency.

He is Rod "The Bod," a male stripper.

Sam meets a beautiful cocktail waitress, Dianna, and smiles, but she doesn't respond. Sam finds out that she is deaf.

Al informs Sam that he will have to "shake his booty," as Rod for another twenty-four hours. Sam doesn't know if he can last that long.

Sam's here to save Dianna, who is an incredible dancer even though she is deaf.

If Sam doesn't convince her she can have this career, she will continue as a hooker and die of AIDS in 1986.

This episode guest starred Debbie Allen, who also directed and choreographed.

Original airdate: March 20, 1991

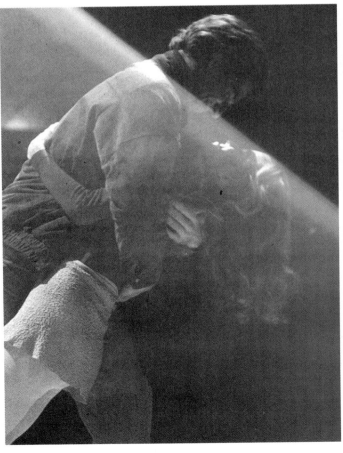

124

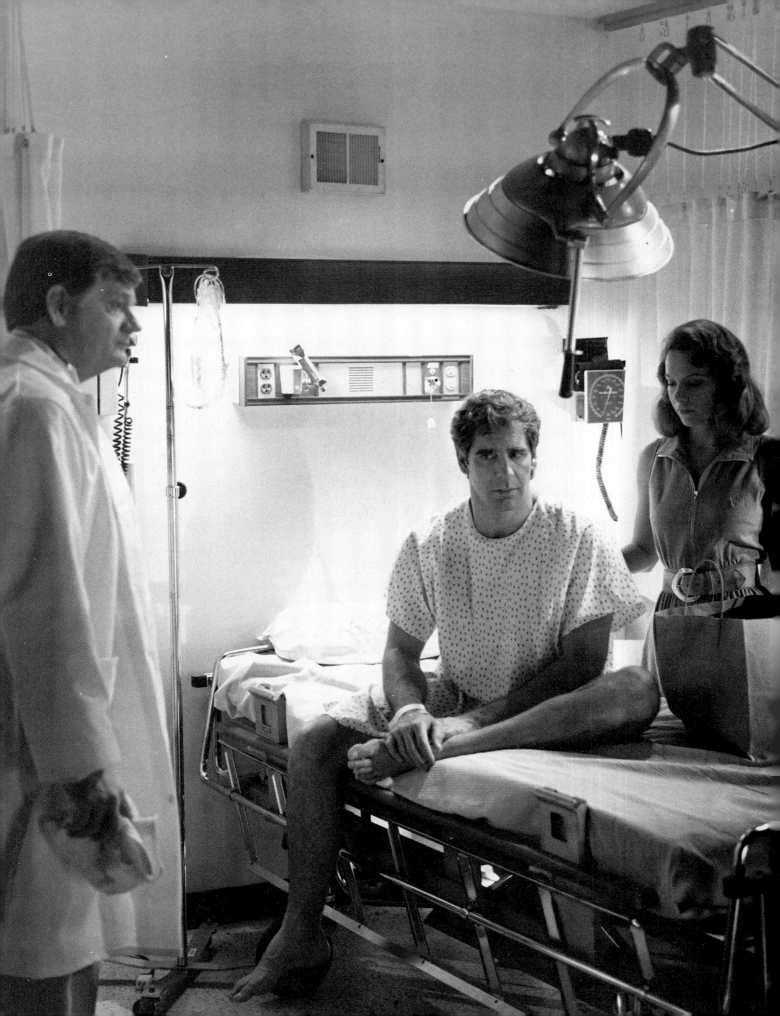

"RAPED," JUNE 20, 1980
Written by Beverly Bridges
Directed by Michael Zinberg

Sam leaps into Katie O'Donoghue right after she is examined at the hospital following a brutal rape.

Katie is encouraged by police officer Shumway to press charges against Kevin Wentworth, who raped her after their third date. Her parents and sister, though outraged, are not supportive, especially after a humiliating article in the local newspaper.

Officer Shumway convinces D.A. Nancy Hudson to put out a warrant for the socially prominent Wentworth.

Sam doesn't see how he can testify about an event he didn't experience, and the real Katie, back in the imaging chamber, is still catatonic and can be of no help.

Ziggy discovers not only that Wentworth will end up running his father's liquor store and will abuse women, but that Katie will commit suicide.

Ziggy says Sam must testify, and hunts for a psychiatric report made shortly before Katie killed herself. The hybrid computer also finds that Wentworth beat up a girlfriend shortly before his date with Katie, but the police haven't connected the two assaults.

During the trial, the ex-girlfriend recants and Wentworth is convincing in his denials. Katie is imaged back to her real time to testify in the nick of time.

Wentworth is convicted but released on his own recognizance to prepare his appeal. When he waylays Sam/Katie, Sam's strength turns the tables and Wentworth is wheeled away on a stretcher.

Al reports that Kevin Wentworth gets the maximum sentence and that Katie recovers and becomes a D.A.

Original airdate: October 30, 1991

"ANOTHER MOTHER," SEPTEMBER 30, 1981
Written by Deborah Pratt
Directed by Joe Scanlan

A serene setting: A sunny kitchen in a modest home. Sam is standing at the stove stirring oatmeal. Kids sit at a table arguing about who is wearing the others' clothes. Calm quickly turns to chaos.

Sam thinks he must be a father and wonders if it is ever easy for a parent. Then he discovers he's not a father. He's Mom!

Sam is the divorced mother of three. He has to try to teach the fifteen-year-old the right attitude and respect for any kind of intimate behavior. It's nearly mpossible to convince a fifteen-yar-old of anything. The kid seems doomed by peer pressure. In the original history, he's killed by pedophilic kidnappers. Sam must save him.

This is the first episode in which we learn that children under the age of five can see Al, because of their innocence.

Original airdate: January 10, 1990

SHOULD BE:
January 27, 1982

"ROBERTO!" JANUARY 26, 1982
Written by Chris Ruppenthal
Directed by Scott Bakula

Sam leaps into the body of Roberto Guttierrez, a television talk-show host in New Mexico investigating the source of deadly gases being produced at a pesticide plant.

Sam and Jani Eisenberg, a young reporter, interview a local man who claims to have seen aliens. Jani also receives a call from another man, saying three of his sheep disappeared the same day his neighbor spotted the extraterrestrials.

An employee at the pesticide plant calls Sam/Roberto, to meet immediately, but enroute Sam and Jani find that the employee's dead. Sam finds his work ID card nearby.

At the pesticide plant, Sam and Jani find bulky safety suits that might be mistaken for aliens. Sam knows that the plant manufactures some type of nerve gas that could kill sheep and that the men in protective suits are being sent to retrieve the dead animals.

When he and Jani go into the plant with a camera crew, the incriminating protective gear is gone. Sam's boss at the station demands that he apologize to the plant's manager, Saxton, so Sam invites him to be his on-air guest for a public apology.

Via their newsroom computer, Sam and Jani access the plant's computer and discover they're making a deadly gas that is fatal to humans.

While Sam and Jani camp out in the newsroom in an effort to trap Saxton, a mysterious man enters and replaces Jani's asthma inhaler with an identical one filled with the poison.

On-air, Sam takes out Jani's inhaler and asks Saxton if this is the ideal way to kill someone who's exposing secrets. Sam squirts the inhaler in Saxton's face and the plant manager panics, yelling "You've killed us all!"

Sam tells him he's about to be arrested for the employee's murder and the attempted murder of Jani.

Original airdate: March 11, 1992

"PERMANENT WAVE," JUNE 2, 1983
Written by Beverly Bridges
Directed by Scott Bakula

Sam leaps into Frank Bianca, owner of a Beverly Hills hair salon, and must save the lives of Frank's girlfriend, Laura, and her young crippled son, Kyle, who witnessed the murder of the pharmacist next door.

That night, Al reports that mother and son will die in two days in Arrowhead, where Frank has a cabin. Kyle must identify the killer, so Sam questions the boy and deduces that the pharmacist was shot while backing out of a drug deal.

A shot grazes Chloe, the salon receptionist, when she comes for a visit. While searching the pharmacy for clues, Sam finds a penny from a penny loafer. Back home, he discovers that a frightened Laura has taken off with Kyle for Arrowhead.

Ziggy reports that mother and son will die that very night, so Al monitors the situation, transporting himself from car to car, and discovers that a police detective, who has been investigating the case, wears penny loafers.

When Laura and Kyle reach the hideaway, the cop is waiting for them. He knocks out Laura and goes after the boy. Sam shows up, trying to protect Kyle, but the cop gets the drop on them.

When the cop is about to shoot, he's killed by Chloe, who explains that she hired him as a drug middleman to sell to the salon's wealthy customers. Before she can murder them, Sam guns her down with the cop's weapon.

Al reports that Frank and Laura will marry and that Frank will train Kyle to become an Olympic athlete.

Original airdate: October 16, 1991

"TEMPTATION EYES," FEBRUARY 1, 1985
Written by Paul Brown
Directed by Chris Hibler

Sam leaps into Dylan Powell, a San Francisco television newsman being tipped off by a serial killer after each murder. A beautiful psychic, Tamlyn Matsuda, identifies a man connected with the latest murder and Sam must save her from being the next victim.

At the scene of the most recent murder, Sam/Dylan and his partner Ross Taylor meet Tamlyn, who has a mental picture of a thin, long-haired man entering the window.

Al says that Dylan is close to retirement and his career had been going downhill until the killer began to call. In two weeks, on Valentine's Day, Tamlyn will be his next victim.

Sam is skeptical about Tamlyn's psychic powers until she calls him by his real name and senses Al's presence in the room.

The next day, at the police station, Tamlyn sees a mug shot of the man she sensed the night before in the murder victim's apartment.

That night, Tamlyn sees Sam as he really is in his mirror image: She recognizes him from a dream in which he saved her from drowning. Sam suspects it is a premonition of her own death.

Over Al's protests, Sam tells her that he has leaped from the future to save her. They make love and, later, he tells her about his time-travel adventures.

On Valentine's Day, the killer calls, saying Tamlyn will be the next victim. Al reports it will happen in Chinatown, where Sam/Dylan, Ross and Tamlyn drive to confront fate.

Tamlyn can feel the killer everywhere. She sees the man in the mug shot, but after Sam catches him, Al says that Tamlyn still dies.

Tamlyn and Ross are alone and she has a mental picture of him killing a prostitute. Realizing he's the serial killer, she tries to run, but he drags her into an alley.

Ziggy discovers that Ross is the killer. After a chase through Chinatown, Sam finds Tamlyn and Ross, who contends that he's been killing for ratings. Ross jumps to his death and Sam, who loves Tamlyn, leaps.

Original airdate: January 22, 1992

"DOCTOR RUTH," APRIL 25, 1985
Written by Robin Jill Bernheim
Directed by Stuart Margolin

Sam finds himself in New York as Dr. Ruth Westheimer. Al believes that Sam has jumped to play matchmaker to mismatched Debbie and Doug, the producer and announcer of Dr. Ruth's radio show, who are always bickering but very much in love. But Sam is sure he must help Annie, a caller on the show, whose boss, Jonathan, a lawyer, is hitting on her. At a book signing, Sam/Dr. Ruth meets Annie, who explains how Jonathan hounds her since taking her out once after work. Then she sees him in the bookstore watching them, and she runs off.

In the Chamber, Al tells Dr. Ruth that he needs to love many women at a time, which she analyzes as fear of being abandoned: as a child he was probably left alone. He admits he grew up in an orphanage. Sam/Dr. Ruth valiantly attempts to keep Doug and Debbie together, but they break up. Now Doug must be stopped from ruining his life, and misdirecting Debbie's by running off with another woman who only wants to use him. Annie calls for help during a radio show because Jonathan is trying to break into her apartment. Sam/Dr. Ruth rushes to her aid and finds her unconscious from gas fumes. When he revives her, she can only remember fainting, and can't be sure if she inadvertently turned

the gas on herself. Sam/Dr. Ruth convinces Annie to quit her job, and while they are clearing out her desk, Jonathan arrives and contends that Annie has been hounding him and became unstable when he wouldn't leave his wife.

During the next show, Al senses that Annie is in trouble. He warns Sam, who manipulates the callers to discuss Debbie and Doug, succeeding in bringing the couple back together, then rushes over to Annie's apartment as Jonathan is attempting to rape her. Sam/Dr. Ruth knocks him out. Annie goes on to become a lawyer specializing in sexual harassment and Doug and Debbie get married. Sam leaps after Dr. Ruth makes Al say the words "I love you" to his girlfriend, Tina.

Original airdate: January 19, 1993

"MOMENTS TO LIVE," MAY 4, 1985
Written by Tommy Thompson
Directed by Joe Napolitano

Sam leaps into Lyle Hart, a soap-opera star who plays a doctor on "Moments to Live."

Sam must go on a dinner date with Norma Pilcher, a fan who won a contest and is madly in love with him. After dinner, she pulls a gun and forces Sam/Lyle inside her motor home, where her husband, Hank, is waiting.

They then go to her mother's house, where the mother tells Sam/Lyle that he's going to get Norma pregnant. He's knocked out and when he comes to, he is shackled to a wall.

Al discovers that Norma's "mother" is really her former roommate at a psychiatric hospital; her real mother overdosed on drugs.

Norma attempts to seduce Sam, infuriating her husband. While they argue, Sam escapes, but Hank recaptures him.

Sam convinces Hank that Norma needs help. When Hank fakes a heart attack, Sam orders Norma to get a knife, so he can perform surgery. She realizes Sam isn't a real doctor, that it was all a setup and she runs to the river, intending to jump off the bridge.

Sam catches her, convinces her not to jump and to get professional help.

Original airdate: April 8, 1992

"PIANO MAN," NOVEMBER 10, 1985
Written by Deborah Pratt
Directed by James Whitmore, Jr.

In a smoke-filled bar, Sam finds himself sitting at a well-worn piano. The rhythm machine thunks next to him, while a shallow bass line repeats the same four-bar phrase.

Sam is Chuck Tanner, a lounge performer. A flirtatious lady asks him to play her a special song. Sam hastily finds the music and sings. There's not a dry eye in the house.

Sam not only must prevent the murder of his klutzy partner Lorraine, but also make Chuck and Lorraine a successful lounge act or their future is hopeless.

Original airdate: March 27, 1991

"REVENGE OF THE EVIL LEAPER," SEPTEMBER 16, 1987
Written by Deborah Pratt
Directed by Debbie Allen

Sam hypnotizes Alia, so she can't be tracked down by Lothos, her computer. Al pops in to inform Alia she's Angel Jenson, and that she's leaped with Sam. She is in jail for selling marijuana. Al says that Sam has leaped to keep Liz Tate from being executed for killing Carol Benning. Zoey has leaped into the body of Warden Meyers to talk to Fiddler, who was an accomplice when Carol was killed. When Sam/Liz and Alia/Angel prove to be uncooperative, Zoey/Meyers puts them back into isolation. Al tells Sam that there is an evil leaper who is after Alia, and that Alia has residual memories of Angel so Lothos can't lock in on her. Sam/Liz talks to Fiddler to try to straighten out the facts. Al tells him that Fiddler vanished after she was released from prison in a case of mistaken identity.

Sophie informs Sam/Liz that the warden wants to see her, and Al interrupts to say he's learned both Liz and Angel now die. The prison officials tie Alia/Angel to the wall so she'll talk. Sam/Liz hears Alia/Angel's screams and knocks out a security guard to release her. Al tells Sam/Liz if he can get Vivian (a security guard) to help, then there is a 91 percent chance they'll get over the wall and be able to escape. Sam explains to Vivian that he and Alia are time travelers and not Liz and Angel. He also warns Vivian that Zoey/Warden Meyers is an evil time traveler. Zoey/Meyers finds Sam/Liz and Alia/Angel and gets ready to shoot them. As Zoey shoots, Alia is taken away by a red Quantum Wash, and the real Angel appears. Vivian shoots Zoey/Meyers because he was responsible for Carol's death. Carol and Meyers were having an affair. When she became pregnant and began to hemorrhage, he let her bleed to death. Warden Meyers is charged, Liz and Angel are paroled, and Vivian heads the prison.

Original airdate: February 23, 1993

"LEAP BACK" JUNE 15, 1945
Written by Donald P. Bellisario
Directed by Michael Zinberg

Al and Sam have "simo-leaped," exchanging places after being struck by lightning.

Al has now leaped into the body of Captain Tom Jarret, a war hero and former POW, returning home to Crown Point, Indiana, in 1945. Sam is the Observer.

A beautiful young woman embraces Al/Tom in a cafe. She's Susanne, his former fiancée, who's about to be married to Clifford White.

Sam/the Observer is unable to enter the Imaging Chamber without a functioning handlink, but by mailing a letter to Gushie, the head engineer, with instructions that it's not to be opened until 1999, he's able to override the computer.

Once in the Control Center, Sam greets his comrades for the first time since he began time traveling four years before. He realizes that he's married—to his one-time fiancée, Dr. Donna Eleese.

After being reprogrammed, Ziggy learns that Al is in Crown Point in 1945 to prevent Al/Tom and Susanne from committing suicide.

When Sam leaps back in, Al and Susanne are at Lovers Leap, where they plan to kill themselves that night. Susanne walks away; there's a scream and Al runs after her.

Clifford appears and knocks out Al, too. He plans to put Al and Susanne into their car and push them over the cliff, making it appear a suicide.

Sam has no choice but to leap back in as Tom, reversing the simo-leap.

As Clifford is about to push the car into the abyss, Sam leaps in and punches him, knocking him over the edge.

Original airdate: September 18, 1991

135

THE MANY LOOKS OF *LEAP*:
A Conversation With the Production Designer

It's not your average television series, with the same two or three "standing" sets, episode after episode, sometimes year in and year out.

Think of Archie's living room from *All in the Family*, the *M*A*S*H* mess tent, or that homey place "where everybody knows your name," the Boston pub in *Cheers*.

But *Quantum Leap,* which weekly careens through time and space—from the early fifties to the future, from neon-lit Las Vegas to the jungles of Vietnam—doesn't have that luxury, even though the "look" of each episode is crucial to its believability.

Enter the production designer.

Cameron Birnie, a veteran of television production design even though he's still in his thirties, has been *Quantum Leap*'s designer since the pilot episode, but because of his youth he almost didn't get the job.

"At that time I was thirty-four or thirty-five," Birnie said. The show's creator, Don Bellisario, admitted, "Frankly, I was hoping to get someone older, because this is a period show and it goes down all the way to the fifties. I was looking for someone who lived through the fifties."

"The only reason I got the show," Birnie recalled, "is that I convinced him that the way we do everything these days is to research it, so it doesn't matter if you lived through it or not."

With only a single week until the pilot was scheduled to shoot, Birnie was hired. He still remembers the pilot episode as the hardest one he's ever done.

In it, Sam and Al and the basic premise of the "leap" are all introduced, and Sam makes his very first leap, becoming a 1950s test pilot who's scheduled to fly the experimental X-2 rocket plane and, for the first time, break the Mach-3 barrier.

"The hardest thing was the pilot episode, particularly the X-2 rocket," Birnie said. "Evidently Don served time in the service and he knows a lot about testing rockets in the fifties. He knew exactly what the X-2 was, exactly what it looked like.

"He said, 'Don't worry, we'll get one,' and we went down to the Air Museum in Chino and looked through all their stuff and they didn't have it.

"It became apparent that we weren't going to get one

QUANTUM LEAP
WARD 6
&
NURSES STATION

anywhere. So then we went to the next thing which was called a V-1 rocket, which was the Navy version of the Air Force X-2, and we came to [Don] with a proposed plan on how we would turn the Navy V-1 rocket into the Air Force X-2 rocket."

But Bellisario, known as a stickler for detail, "didn't go for it. He said there were too many differences. He said, 'I can tell, and if I can tell other people can tell.' So what I had to do to get it ready, because there were only four or five days left, was come up with this new way of doing things.

"We decided to make [the X-2] out of foam. Basically, it's a giant surf board, carved out of foam and fiberglass. What we did is, we got a lot of pictures of what the X-2 rocket looked like and we got a foam carver, and the foam carver

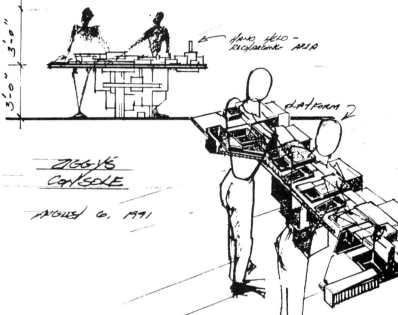

ZIGGY'S
CONSOLE

AUGUST 6, 1991

glued tons of blocks, giant blocks of foam together, and then we gave him overall dimensions—forty feet long, the wing span, the whole bit. We had him sculpt the X-2 rocket."

How did Birnie know a foam-sculpted X-2 rocket plane would work? "I've worked with [foam carvers] before. I did a feature called *The Golden Child* [starring Eddie Murphy], where they used giant Buddhas [carved out of foam].

"Basically, the X-2 was built in a week and shipped up to Edwards Air Force Base. When you saw it flying, you either saw the cockpit area against rear-screen projection, or you saw stock footage [i.e., footage from film libraries]. Anytime you saw it in the air it was a real one."

But that's not the only innovation Birnie came up with for the pilot episode. "I had the opportunity to redesign a Ferrari," he said gleefully, referring to the futuristic automobile Al is driving when he stops to pick up a lovely blond hitchhiker in the pilot episode's opening scene. "They brought in a Testarrosa Ferrari [but originally] they wanted a Lamborghini Countache."

But the Lamborghini "didn't work out because the windows didn't roll down," and, in the scene, Al rolls down the window to talk to the hitchhiker, stranded beside her own broken-down car by the side of the road. "So we went to our second choice, which was the Testarrosa Ferrari.

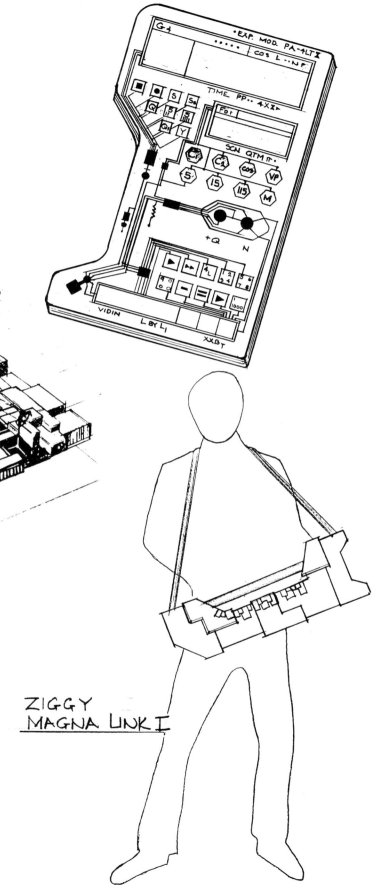

ZIGGY
MAGNA LINK I

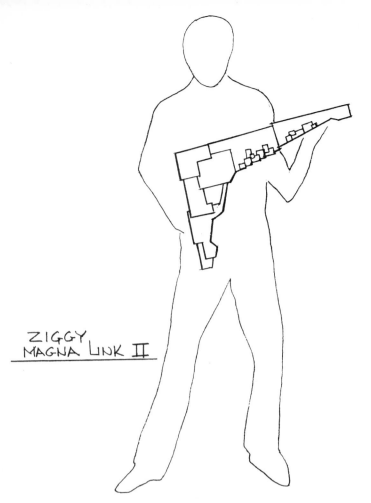

ZIGGY
MAGNA LINK II

"We redesigned the front bumper system and the rear bumper system. We made it like a solid light bar and we added pieces here and there to make it slightly different . . . and we added a glowing star hood ornament."

Paradoxically, it's the show's futuristic sets that have always presented a particular challenge for the production designer. "The handlink [which Al uses to communicate with Ziggy, the computer] was actually designed twice," Birnie said. "It was designed [one way] for the first season, but Don's instructions were that he wanted it very futuristic, but he wanted it unidentifiable.

"He doesn't want people to dwell too much on it, he doesn't want people to recognize it in any way.

"These concepts are very difficult to sell to Don. We must go through ten design concepts before he finally settles on something.

"The handlink he had me redesign in the second season. What it ended up with is just colored cubes put together, which finally achieved what he wants.

"The control room [of the Quantum Project] was similar. I expanded on the handlink. The control console and some of the props are just enlarged handlinks, bigger cubes, and the wall we used was actually a waterfall wall, so we actually had water running down the angled wall of the set."

But the oddest thing the production designer ever had to envision was an ocean-going trash compacter, for an episode set aboard the *Queen Mary*. It was "one of the strangest things I ever did," he remembered. "They wrote a story about being on the *Queen Mary* and one of the rescues was when Sam gets thrown into this giant garbage-compacter room.

"It really doesn't exist on the *Queen Mary*. What we wanted was this room where they're dumping all this trash and when it gets full they have this giant hydraulic push arm that pushes all this trash out through an opening into the ocean.

"What we ended up doing is building this giant trash chute and it was pushed by a fork lift. [Actually] it was a wall on the end of a fork lift that moved through this tunnel, and then the opening had to angle down into this pit, and we had to put a giant blue screen down there because later they added onto the blue screen the ocean traveling underneath."

The "blue screen" is a way of melding a live foreground character with filmed background action; it's the same technique that TV weatherpersons use when they stand in front of a map with swirling clouds.

But not all backgrounds are as serious as that. Take, for example, the episode called "The Curse of Ptah-Hotep," in which Sam is in Egypt, excavating a pharaoh's tomb.

The tomb, constructed on Universal Studios' cavernous Stage 17, is decorated with authentic-looking hieroglyphics. And, as producer Chris Ruppenthal points out, most of the hieroglyphics *are* authentic. He hired a prominent academic, an Egyptologist from Berkeley, to consult for the episode and to render into ancient Egyptian the pharaoh's curse *(As for anyone who will disturb the tomb of the King Ptah-Hotep. . . death will swallow him!).*

But among the ancient cartouches and hieroglyphs are some droll modern touches: Rolling Stone tongues, one pharaoh in a line of pharaohs who's discreetly smoking a cigarette and, most incongruous of all—Bart Simpson!

"That was the set painters," Birnie admitted ruefully. "They have a sense of humor and they start doing those things [as a joke] . . . I'm hoping nobody [in the home audience] sees that stuff."

So now you've been warned.

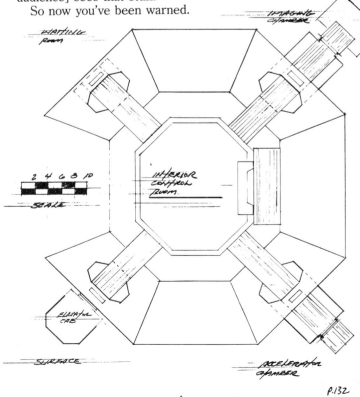

INTERIOR CONTROL ROOM

SET CONSTRUCTION ESTIMATE
UNIVERSAL CITY STUDIOS, INC.

Date: 8-7-91

Show: Quantum Leap

Estimate By: [signature]

Prod. No.: 67303

Art Director: C. Be____

Set Title: Univ. Accelerator Chamber

Set No.: 1 Location: 7

Departments	Propmakers	Grips	Paint	Staff	Total
LAYOUT:	435	70	125	20	650
SCAFFOLD-FOOTAGE: Scaffold camera platform		2500			2500
BACKINGS-TOTAL		300			300
ROLL CEILING-TOTAL:					
NEW WALLS-SQ FT: 2970	7175		2870	600	10645
STOCK WALLS-					
WINDOWS, NEW:					
WINDOWS, STOCK:					
OPENINGS:					
DOOR, NEW:					
DOORS, STOCK:					
FIREPLACES, NEW:					
FIREPLACES, STOCK:					
CABINETS, NEW:					
TRIM:	700				700
TOUCH UP & TIE -IN:					
center platform 300 #	1050		350		1400
5 Ramps	1440		360		1800
Elevation cab 30 Fly	300		200	40	540
4 doors + openings	2000		200		2200
4 Tunnel 120' lg	4800		1200	240	6240
HARDWARE:					
SIGNS	600	600			1200
FLOOR:					
LABOR (724):	3470				3470
STOCK UNITS (727):					
GREENS:					
MISC. DEPTS:	55				55
TOTAL LABOR:	4125	18500	2870	5305	900	31700

BUDGET		STRIKE:	
LABOR 3300		MATERIAL:	
STRIKE		TOTAL:	
MATERIALS			
TOTAL			

EXECUTIVE APPROVAL _____ DATE _____

FORM 4716 (REV. 3/91)

· QUANTUM LEAP ·
5HOCK THERAPY ROOM

FALLOUT SHELTER.
THE NUCLEAR FAMILY — QUANTUM LEAP.

WHAT THE WELL-DRESSED TIME TRAVELER WEARS: A Conversation With the Costume Designer

Far from the tourist trams and the Universal tour, in a distant corner of the vast Universal City film and television studio, is a nondescript four-story building that looks like a factory, with a loading dock and a small fleet of trucks parked nearby.

On its top floor is the Universal Costume Department, and in a small corner office, crowded with period hats and jewelry, with sketches and movie posters on the walls, sits Jean-Pierre Dorleac, the dapper Emmy Award-winning and Oscar-nominated veteran costume designer. He's been dressing the *Quantum* cast since the beginning. How did he get involved?

"I've worked for Don [Bellisario] for fourteen years. We got started together on *Battlestar Gallactica*." Dorleac recalled. "He was a line producer and a writer and a director, and he wrote the script for 'The Man with the Thousand Lives' that guest-starred Fred Astaire, that I ended up winning the Emmy [for costume design].

"Since then, he's called me on *Airwolf, Tales of the Gold Monkey*, some *Magnum*s and a series that wasn't [made] called *The Ultimate Adventure Company*. Then he called me to do specifically Dean and Scott."

The series' two leads have their own approaches to their costumes. "Dean doesn't like fittings. We haven't had a fitting for Dean in years," Dorleac said. With Scott Bakula, "Even when it comes down to doing the women's clothing that he was to wear, he's very professional. He puts it on and goes to work."

The show has evolved its own complexities, Dorleac observed. "Television is never easy, because of the time frame you have to work in," he said. "In a regular series, like *Designing Women* or *Murphy Brown*, the designers generally create what is known as a 'closet' for the leading characters, and that consists of a hundred pieces to create a different look everytime.

"We can't do that with *Quantum Leap*. Dean repeats his clothes; Scott doesn't—a new time frame, a new location every episode."

That creates its own imperatives. "We may do 1957 four times within a year, but we do it in various locales and climates and different times of the year, and so the look always changes."

That look can get very specific. "We know when pantyhose came in 1958, and if we're doing the South in 1960, and it's a small town, we'll still put ladies in seamed hosiery," Dorleac explains, "because it wasn't that influential. But if we're doing New York [in the same year], then all the ladies have got to have hosiery that has no seams in the back.

"The same thing with flares and bell-bottom trousers— how [influential] they were in 1969, as opposed to 1972. Men's collars and tie widths, all that kind of thing. When you can use polyester, and when you can't."

Anything else would be unfair to the audience, said Dorleac. "It's feeding them misinformation."

And some of the best information, he added, comes from the fans themselves. "We have wonderful fans who send us things. It's endearing.

"I get hats and fur stoles and shoes and old suits in from people all the time. 'This is my grandmother's hat. Could you let somebody wear it in the show, because I'd love to see it.' And it's quite charming."

What's equally charming is what happens next. "I probably get two or three boxes of costumes every week, and we use them," Dorleac says. "We got in a box of things from Clovis, New Mexico, last week and we turned around and used four of the dresses in the Las Vegas show [then shooting]. It's new, it's fresh, it hasn't been used on screen before."

JEAN-PIERRE DORLÉAC
·91·

GREAT SCOTT:
A Conversation With
Scott Bakula

In a business where jealousy, backbiting and gossip-mongering are endemic, it's impossible to find anyone who dislikes actor Scott Bakula.

Ask any of the *Quantum Leap* cast or crew and you hear the same comments: "complete pro," "multi-talented," "easy-going," "the glue that holds the whole thing together."

Old-pro technicians, a relatively cynical lot, seem in awe of his energy level and marvel that he spends lunch hours organizing softball games or rollerblading around the set. Assistant directors point out how little direction Bakula requires and that he does his own stunts, regularly getting banged up in the process. Bit-part actresses, on call for only a single day, talk of his courtesy and consideration.

It seems hard to believe, until to you talk to the guy.

Let's start at the beginning: how'd you get into the show, how'd you get the part?

My agent called me, said there was a new show by Don Bellisario. I didn't know him, he didn't know me at all. One of the casting persons knew me and had asked that I come in.

The most remarkable thing about getting the show was that it happened very quickly by Hollywood standards. I got this phone call on a Tuesday. They said they were going to send me the script: they ended up sending me two scenes. I called my agent, said, "Where's the script?" He said, "Well, it's not done."

So I got these two scenes [from the pilot] and they were terrific. There's the scene where I see Al when I'm fishing with my kid and he comes by; and the car scene where I'm driving with my wife home from the bar, where we start talking about life and stuff.

I read for the role. That night, all of a sudden, the full script was done and I got it.

Thursday, I went back and met everybody at the Tower [the "Black Tower," as Universal's high-rise headquarters is known in Hollywood]. I read for it again [in front of the Universal Television executives].

Friday, I went to the network [to meet the NBC executives]. Friday afternoon the deal was negotiated and Friday night it was done.

A couple weeks later, we were shooting. It was fast.

What attracted you to the show?

I loved the writing. It constantly surprised me.

What did you bring to the part?

I think I gave the show an opportunity to expand beyond what it might have been—because of my theatrical background, because of my athletic background....It still would've worked with stunt doubles, but I think it's more interesting knowing it's me.

They've been able to create kind of a huge background and biography for Sam. You know: He played the piano for a while and couldn't decide if he wanted to be a piano player; he played basketball with his brother.

And a lot of that was me.

When I was growing up, I did many, many things—to the point where my Dad finally said, "You've got to start picking, you can't play six sports a year. It doesn't work that way."

What's the hardest thing you ever had to on the show?

The most physically difficult was the trapeze, because I have motion sickness. So, not only was I swinging back and forth, but I was hanging upside down for hours. I was sick most of that time.

I had needles in my ears and acupressure and stuff; I tried everything.

You ever consider just having a stunt double do it?

Well, we had cameras up in the air. The leap-in was me swinging back and forth, upside down. There was no way you could leap anybody else in. It had to be me. I mean, we had three- or four-page scenes on the trapeze.

What's the toughest role you ever played for the show?

I think the role in "Shock Theatre" last year was the most challenging role for me.

It was the most exhilarating and fulfilling of anything I've done for the show, because it gave me a chance to actually, for a few minutes, become these people, instead of just being Sam inside these people. I actually got to assume their personalities.

The pregnancy episode was extremely challenging.

Do you research the characters? Did you go talk to pregnant women?

Well, I had my wife. Her pregnancy was very vivid to me. Many of the things I did in that episode were direct rip-offs of things that she'd felt and her behavior during her pregnancy.

But what I try and do with the show is—and that is a totally different approach than I've ever done before—I try and *not* know. I try to do as little research as I have to.

Obviously, if I have to fly on a trapeze, I have to go train and then I have to *un*learn it. Or if I have to box, I have to go train to box and then I have to *un*learn it.

But, most recently, when I was in the episode with the all-girl singing group, the leap-in was the middle of an opening number. And I said [to them], "You can do whatever you want—practice, rehearse, whatever—but

when you're ready to shoot, I'll just come out and do it."

So, I didn't have a clue where they were going, what they were going to do, and I just found my way through it. That's the nature of Sam—every week he's improvising—so I try not to know.

Is there something inside, a clue to the character of Sam, something the audience doesn't know?

Yeah... but it's not something I'd tell. You want to let Sam have a little mystery. In many ways he's a bit of an open book. His life has been so simple.

My biggest thing about Sam is that I think emotionally he's pretty young. Anytime you go through school in the manner he did—you graduate high school at sixteen, you graduate college at eighteen and MIT by twenty-one—you have no time to live.

It's like young athletes and young actors, they don't have a life. They're too busy working.

Emotionally, Sam has got a lot to learn about life. That's what I think has been fun for him, in terms of the series, that he's been exposed to things he never would've been exposed to. He might've heard about them or read about them, but this is a guy who's been locked in a cave in New Mexico and only comes out for meals basically, because he's a scientist and he's totally locked into what he's doing. So it's been great to watch Sam grow.

Can you articulate how he's grown, other than what you've just said?

I think he's much more accepting of different aspects of the world than he was in the beginning. I think he's much less shockable. I think he's quicker now to adapt. I certainly think he's much quicker in his guises; it's much easier now to fall into something.

He's a much better undercover leaper than he was in the beginning.

The trick for me as an actor is to maintain enough of the quandary and enough of the humor of a lot of his leaps. I don't want it to get easy for Sam.

I think his relationship with Al has changed a lot. There're a lot of holes in their history, which will someday be answered, I hope.

The two of them have become much better friends. Their early relationship was revolving around almost a codependency. Sam depended on Al at an early point in his life, and then Al went down hill and was in trouble and Sam pulled him out, and Al came to depend a little bit on him. Now, they've become almost equal through this leaping.

Do you have a favorite period to leap into?

We've gone from '52 until the present and all the way up to '99.

I really like a lot of stories from the fifties and the early sixties. I find that stylistically the most interesting, visually the most interesting.

I think that most of the stories could be told in any decade. I'm hoping that the stories are universal enough and timeless enough, [so] that they could also play in Russia, play in England, in Australia. That seems to be happening.

What do you think it is about the show that appeals to people—the science fiction, the nostalgia, the retro aspects, the issues you deal with?

I think it's all those things. The show offers so much and at the same time, I feel, is unpretentious about it.

How many episodes have you directed?

Just two.

What's the most unexpected thing about directing?

I just really liked working with the actors, more than I thought I would. I think I had fear about that, about being able to communicate.

I really enjoyed the one-on-one connection. I'm an actor who tends to be very polite in the workplace. I don't interfere with the director and his relationship with the other actors.

So when I was directing, it was just great to get right to the other actors, in a sense, without a director in the way. It eliminated one person from the chain.

Do you write as well?

Yes, but not formally. Not as yet.

What's been your input on the character?

Very early on I had input in that I wanted Sam to be a little more serious than they did. I wanted him to be a little straighter.

There was a sense in the beginning that Sam wasn't funny enough. As I tried to explain to them at the time—successfully; fortunately they listened to me, because the alternative, really, would've been probably just to replace me—I didn't want to do, like, Billy Murray's Sam Beckett, which would've been a totally different guy.

My feeling was, I like to believe these things. I like to believe that time travel is possible, I like to believe in holograms and all that stuff. I feel like scientifically it's possible, we just haven't done it yet, but someday it'll happen.

To hook an audience, and get them to suspend [disbelief] and come with us, I had to be totally serious and honest about what we were doing. Every scene that I looked at, whether there were comedic elements to it or not, I wanted to present in that fashion.

Sometimes you can betray an audience, by coming out of nowhere to tell a joke or something, and they're expecting you to behave one way and you don't. Now, a lot of times you want to do that, you want to surprise them.

You know, Dean has so many wonderful comedic bits to do, I didn't feel it was necessary for me to be scoring with jokes and double takes and things like that. I do a lot of funny things on the show, but it isn't exactly what they were looking for in the beginning.

What do you think the chemistry is between you and Dean?

You never know what's going to happen in something like this.

I read with Dean when he came in to the network and we hit it off from the beginning. Who knew that when we would get to do this, we'd feel psychologically the same about a lot of things? So, we're connected on how we want the show to be, *what* we want the show to be. There's no infighting over that. He has no ego about his work or my work.

It's almost like having a brother-situation, only without the fights. We just don't fight.

Beyond the work, we enjoy each other's company, we enjoy each other's families and kids.

Did you ever think the show would last this long?

No. I'm surprised every day that we come to work that somebody hasn't said, What's the show doing on the air?

Now, the fans "get it," but it seems to me the network never "got it" and Hollywood, the Business, doesn't "get it" either.

How do you mean?

As I hear it, the network didn't get the concept at the beginning, and to this day, if they could figure out a way to get the viewers to tune into something else, you'd be gone. But you're like *Star Trek* used to be: You have those loyal viewers, and they can't ignore that.

We definitely have been, from day one, a hard sell. You couldn't capsulize the show. It's been extremely difficult to talk about.

The very first time we went to the [network] affiliates and [entertainment] press meetings [to introduce new shows], and [the show's creator] Don [Bellisario] would say, "This is what the show is about," people were just dumbfounded.

You know, they couldn't believe this was going on the air; they couldn't imagine what it was going to be about; they couldn't figure out what Dean Stockwell was doing there. Here's a guy with an Academy Award nomination, and he's playing some hologram! Nobody could figure it out.

All we knew is that Brandon [Tartikoff, former head of NBC] loved the show from the beginning and championed it. They've always been confused about how to market it; it's always kind of found its own way, really.

The fans found it. Actually, the media is what saved us in the beginning, because the press was so good on the show. Fortunately for us, NBC was looking for quality stuff and they were willing to stay with the show for a while.

And in that little interim of time, the fans glommed onto it quick. We developed this following—a small, but sturdy audience that followed us around the schedule—while they were investigating what to do.

Small, sturdy, but a very demographically desirable audience.

We're in the top-five demographic shows on television.

[Note: In this era of fragmented audiences, "demographics"—a measure of audience composition rather than audience size—are often more important than sheer numbers of viewers. Generally, advertisers prefer younger audiences over older audiences.]

Demographically, we're just huge. The numbers issue has changed so much since we started four years ago, in terms of what's acceptable and what's not acceptable, and the demographic thing has become such a huge part of it all. We fit very well demographically; numbers-wise, I'm sure we don't perform as well as they would like us to, but I know that the advertisers love us, and I know that the affiliates love us, because we're leading in to their eleven o'clock news and the right people are watching.

And, like it or not, that's a huge part of what television is.

The advertisers love you until you do a gay-themed episode, until you do an animal-rights episode, until you have a black-and-white romance, until you're a priest. Then they get worried about offending potential customers. Does that cut down on what you can do, or do you do it in their face?

Well, none of it is ever intended to be in anybody's face anyway.

But Don isn't deaf to those issues and he's not deaf to the fact that we need to present a lot of different viewpoints and a lot of different areas of life.

If we just did, you know, Sam leaps into a thirty-five-year-old white male with these seven problems.... Well, you've got to go into all walks of life, all kinds of situations. Some of them have been difficult for our advertisers.

What's encouraging and discouraging at the same time is that there's a group of advertisers who routinely pull out of a show—forget about the particular script—if they hear it's about A, B, C or D. They're just gone. They don't want anything to do with it at all. And, hey, that's their prerogative.

Let's move away from these business questions. Is there any concept you want to do that you haven't done yet?

I'd still love to find a way to do a baby. Financially, it just presents a lot of problems.

Giant sets? Giant furniture and all that?

Yeah, and that becomes a problem, but I'd love to be able to do something along that line.

Issue-wise, there are lots of issue shows. See, it's a good thing that I'm not producing the show, because that's where I would tend [to go].

I'd love us to do a show about the homeless—and it's an easy thing to do; we just haven't found the right show, and Don wants to do it. I'd like to do a show about child abuse. I'd like to do a show about AIDS. And there are several environmental-type shows that we need to do.

My contention is that our audience isn't going to grow much more, but they're going to stay [with us] as long as we're there. So I feel like we have the opportunity—they're so loyal—to almost do anything, and they'll go along. But you have to be careful, you can't abuse an audience.

If we stay true to what the show is all about, we can get into some of these other issues.

You know, we can go to the future.... We can see my death, we can go see Dean's death. There are lots of things that we can get to.

Any bloopers, practical jokes on the set?

Yeah, probably the biggest thing that happened on the set in my memory, we shot a show in which I was in the garbage scow of a big boat.

The shooting took a long time, three days, and the last day I was in it and in it and in it, and, you know, you're just sitting around with garbage on you and you smell for hours.

I thought I was done and they said, "No, no, no. We've got one more shot." And I'm standing there at the end of the day and ten people, including my executive producers, were there with pies—instigated by Dean, of course—so I got pie'd and they left me hanging out in the garbage for two hours, so they could get the shot.

How do you keep your energy level up? You seem to be the spark.

A lot of it is you just get into the habit of it, in terms of what is demanded of your body.

I'm very careful about what I eat during the day. I feel like you have a certain responsibility, and in this case it's not so much a responsibility as it is I'm lucky to be in a position where I can motivate sometimes and play and keep the set light.

I'm determined that all of our guest stars have as good a time as they possibly can. I certainly have been, and certainly will be again, a guest on somebody else's show. It's a very tough thing to do. And when you only have two regulars, it's essential for the show that the guests come in and really feel like they're really the stars of the show.

It's critical that they feel comfortable so that we don't waste a day-and-a-half. In television, that day-and-a-half you never get back.

I hear you rollerblade in the shooting breaks.

I try to.

How did you pick that up?

Actually my daughter is skating a lot, and I skate with her a lot. She's eight.

And the guys [on the crew] were looking for something to give me on my birthday, and the [cast and crew] softball team gave me a whole rollerblade set. So, we all started playing roller hockey.

In three-and-a-half years of shooting, you say there've only been two days when you didn't have to come for one of these twelve- or fourteen-hour shooting days. How do you cope with that pace?

Two years ago, it was four in the morning and I was going into a lake up in the Hollywood Hills.

I had to go into the water and it was forty-five degrees out. The rest of the night involved running through the woods in wet clothes with no shirt on.

I remember turning to somebody and saying, "You know, it's a good thing that I like being here, it's a good thing that I'm with people that I like being with." Because if you weren't, it would be just miserable.

These guys [on the crew] they get me going, too; they lift me up when I'm having problems. They know me pretty well by now. And that's invaluable.

151

THE PRO: A Conversation With Dean Stockwell

If Scott Bakula is *Quantum Leap*'s high-energy sparkplug, then Dean Stockwell is the calm center of the production storm.

After all, this big-screen veteran has been on stage since the age of six, so it's small wonder that the show's co-executive producer calls him a "young old pro."

"If you want to get on Dean's good side," a crew member confides, "ask him about golf. He's a golf maniac."

That's true enough, the visitor learns, sitting with the actor in his Pace Arrow motor home parked near the set. But he's also a serious art collector (although the crowded motor home is mostly decorated with drawings by his children), as well as a perceptive student of the Business.

He's wearing his Observer costume from his last scene—a green and blue suede jacket, a green silk shirt and a green-and-pink striped tie.

The pin on his jacket, a small metal shark wearing pink-stone sunglasses, he picked out himself.

Stockwell puffs Observer-like on a big Chavelo cigar ("It's a prop, actually," he says dryly), pausing thoughtfully before answering questions.

How'd you get the part on *Quantum Leap*?

Welllll, I had asked my agent and the people who were representing me at that time to look for a series, and I was looking at several things. This came about right at that time, and Don Bellisario thought of me.

I read it, I loved it, I went in and met with him and I got the very real impression that he thought that I was the guy to do the role.

Why did you want to do a series? As I remember it, you were flying high in movies, coming off *Blue Velvet* and all that. A lot of people in the Business were surprised that an actor of your stature would take any part in series television.

I wasn't flying that high. I was on an ascendant, there's no question, but I had spent virtually countless years of anxiety wondering whether I was going to get another job all the time, so I wanted a long run at something.

I never thought there was anything wrong with doing a television series. I thought it was a wonderful thing to do, especially since this particular one had what I felt was so much to offer in the way of quality, uniqueness and a wonderful part.

What did you bring to the part?

Well, I brought my talent, whatever that is. I'm not going to describe *that*. That's what I brought to it.

What about insights into the character: Is the character as originally written who you're playing now, or did you bring in little bits of business, little insights of your own?

Both. It's a combination of both. There was a very interesting character to start with. He was, um, very colorful, and he was, um—how shall I put it?—if anything he had an *expanded* appreciation of the opposite gender.

And there was humor in it. I have expanded the humor and expanded the appreciation of the feminine gender, and the writing has gone along with me. I've added a lot of little things and *schticks*, mostly on the comedic side, the light side.

The shows that have dealt with more emotional things, I feel fortunate that they've been few and far between, because I prefer doing the comedy. But those more serious shows have been good ones and well-written, so I have been able to achieve a balance in the performances.

Al seems to me to be a man who's had a real hard life that's tempered him. Is that part of what you brought to the character?

Oh, I wouldn't say that. I don't know that my life has been as hard as his, or maybe it's been more hard. I don't know.

When the situation calls for serious drama...I draw all these things from my imagination; I never research, I never search my soul for experiences that I've had that fit the thing that I'm going to act out. I don't work that way. I work mostly with my mind, and then I'm able to tap into emotions when I actually do it.

Do you have a favorite episode?

I don't. I truly don't.

There will always be a place in my heart for the pilot, because it was the initial experience, and it was a good one—the first time working with Scott, the first time doing the character.

I don't think that was our best episode for sure. It's not. I mean we were fleshing things out, trying to figure out what it was ourselves a little bit.

Apart from that, I would say that all the episodes that have been light—and there have been a lot of them—and funny I have liked the best. Things like the Christmas episode.

Do you have a favorite moment?

My favorite moment usually is the last funny moment that I've found. I get a lot of satisfaction and enjoyment from finding something odd and funny to do.

An example here, today, since we're shooting an episode right at the moment:

We have this scene in a little cafe in the fifties, in New Mexico it's supposed to be—a very-well-designed set by the way—and Sam is playing a stand-up comic and Bob Saget is his partner.... And they kind of get carried away doing a little bit, and the waitress who greeted them as they came in says they're being too crazy and kicks them out.

They go out and I'm supposed to pop out. Well, while they're doing the bit, Sam grabs this red plastic ketchup dispenser, and he uses it like a microphone. And the waitress says to him, "If you're going to be acting crazy and weird like this, you better give me my ketchup and do it someplace else."

So he hands her the ketchup and they go out. I wanted to do a line there, and I thought of going up to her and saying, "Hold the ketchup between your knees"—to do a little homage to Jack [a reference to Jack Nicholson's famous line in *Five Easy Pieces*].

Then, when we actually shot it, I rethought it, 'cause the girl has flaming red hair. So I came up to her and said, "Do you use that stuff on your hair?"

I liked that, I enjoyed doing it and I just did it five minutes ago. And that's my favorite moment until the next one.

That's a good attitude, given the pace and the amount of work you do.

It's a *true* attitude, it's an *organic* attitude.

How do you deal with the pace? You seem pretty mellow, in fact people on the set seem pretty mellow, given this brutal pace.

We know it's hard work, and we know everyone works really hard, but—and this is something that was never discussed, *never* discussed between us—Scott and I, organically, from the beginning, knew the value of creating a certain kind of atmosphere on the set.

An atmosphere that starts with the principal people will permeate the set. If you're all serious and you're all rigid, everything will become that way and you'll have an uptight set.

We both, organically, knew how to keep it loose, and it starts with the banter between Scott and me.

He has that naturally, I have it naturally, and we're both damn lucky that we do, because it just works out wonderfully. And the whole set is constantly loose, but we get the work done and the work is good and on time.

You know, you've got a lot of loyal fans, and it's been my sense that the fans "get" the show, but the Business has never really gotten it.

The Business didn't "get" *Star Trek* either. The Business didn't get it, until the fans just kept after it. That could very well happen with *Quantum Leap*.

I personally feel that *Quantum Leap* will go on and we'll have a fabulous exposure in syndication and that there will be a movie. That's my hunch.

Really? Is it in the works?

I know it's been discussed.

You were in the business since you were a kid. You were in one of my favorite movies.

Really? Which one is that?

The Boy With Green Hair. Tell me, how has the business changed since then?

It's truly the same business. It's the business of entertainment; and hopefully at its best, a provocative and stimulating business, above and beyond the basic entertainment value.

I think entertainment is essential to the human condition, so it is an important endeavor.

The studio system that existed when I was a child fell apart; it doesn't exist anymore. That was a growth in the business

[Note: Under the old "studio system," actors were put under multi-year contracts to individual Hollywood studios, and the studio guided every step of their careers, deciding, for example, in which films they would act, whether they would take acting or other classes, and how their images would be presented to the public.]

I think independent filmmakers brought a great deal to the art form and were freed of the fetters of studio control. More stimulating ideas were brought to the screen. Fewer B-movies as a staple of the studios [were made]. And [there was] just as high a quality of stars. So you can't say that the studio system fostered all these stars, and everything was better because of that. It just simply isn't true.

Television came into the picture. HA! That's funny! I like that. Get it? Television came into the picture!

That's become its own growth industry; a wonderful thing for actors. Unfortunately, the quality across the board isn't consistently very high; it's very commercial.

How did you get into the business? When did you start acting?

I was six, and both my father and mother had been in show business. My father was in musical comedy and we were living in New York. It was about the time that he and my mother were separating, and he'd heard of a play that was casting a bunch of kids in it, so my mother brought my brother and me down to this audition.

She didn't really have a particular reason, she really didn't want us to work. The theater had been her life. She knew it, and it just happened.

So my brother and I got in this play, and then I was seen in it by this talent scout. I did a screen test and was seen in that by MGM and they signed me to a contract. My first picture was *Anchors Aweigh*.

The Boy With Green Hair was a few years later; I was about ten.

Do you have a favorite movie from your career?

Yeah, I have several. *Green Hair* is one of them; it still holds up as a very unique little classic. It says something very important; it's an antiwar film.

There was a picture called *Down to the Sea in Ships* that I did with Richard Widmark and Lionel Barrymore that, for performance, I felt very good about.

A couple of comedies that I did as a kid. Then, later on, *Long Day's Journey Into Night,* with Katharine Hepburn, Ralph Richardson, and Jason Robards. And the film of *Compulsion.*

Then, later on, I would say *Married to the Mob.* I'd put that up as the favorite part I've ever had.

You seem to like word play. Do you write?

No.

Direct?

No. Well, I have. I directed some little theater stuff.

No ambitions in those directions?

Uh-uh.

If you had your choice, is there a *Quantum* you'd like to do that you haven't done?

I've been attempting, over the three-and-a-half years we've been doing this show, to get the production office to do an environmental show. It hasn't happened.

It seems a natural, but...it's a very difficult show to write scripts for.... It's tough to do. No one yet has been able to come up with an environmental script that works.

I feel there is a definite perspective advantage that we have—because we deal with times in the past—to show the origins of the environmental mistakes that have been made, and now to see the consequences.

Is there anything that you know about your character that the audience doesn't know?

No. There are things that come up out of the writers' minds and out of Don's imagination that are unexpected by me and that I adapt to.

A case in point would be [the episode] where the government funding for Project Quantum Leap was going to dry up, and [Sam] changed history with this girl who turned out to be...the senator that's reviewing the project and approves the funding at the last minute.

Al was in some scenes in the present tense at this Senate hearing and, for the first time, out of Don's mind, I was a full admiral. Nobody knew anything about this prior to that episode. All of a sudden, I had to incorporate that into my thinking.

You're a married man with kids. Is this kind of work pace brutal on a family life?

It's a little tough, it's a little tough. I see them mostly on the weekends, because they're not near and it's a long working day—minimum twelve-hour days—but when I'm there it's high-quality time. They come and visit the set from time to time.

It's as good a situation as you could have, given what I'm doing, and I'm doing what I'm doing to provide for their future.

Do your children [aged six and eight] watch the show?

They don't watch it live; it's too late [at night]. There are some episodes that I'd rather they don't see, so we pick and choose the episodes.

What's it like for a six-year-old to see Daddy on screen?

They seem to accept it very readily. They see films from when I was a kid, too. They get right into the stories.... That's the way pure minds work.

They both adore Scott, both personally and on the show.

What do you do between calls on the set?

Quite frequently I have mundane matters to handle here, in this dressing room, my motor home here. Paperwork and stuff.

I enjoy reading. I have a television (with a VCR) here; I watch dailies—dailies, of course, are the rushes that were shot the day before.

I have some weights. Something that I enjoy greatly is a chess computer. I play chess against it. I like that a lot.

Someone said to me I shouldn't leave without asking you about golf.

What about it?

Personally, I don't know anything about it.

Well, I am a golfer. I'm addicted to golf. I think it's the most difficult sport I've ever tried to do. It's the hardest to do, but it's also the most addictive. It's incredibly enjoyable and incredibly frustrating.

I do want to say something [on another topic].

Sure. What's that?

I do want to say that I want to do at least another season on the show, because—and I'm being very honest here—I've been very deeply affected by what I've felt coming back to me from the fans of this show.

I've been very deeply affected by their demeanor, their sincerity, the warmth and affection that they show to the show and to Scott and me.

It's real and I think it's very unique, and I've never experienced that before in my life.

I want them to have twenty-two or forty-four more episodes.

LEAPING AROUND ON LOCATION: A Day With the Cast and Crew

By the general consensus of show business professionals, *Quantum Leap* is the toughest shoot on television.

Unlike other series, *Quantum* has no permanent sets, so each week requires a frenzy of set-building and location shooting.

Because the series leaps through time and space, each week also requires different period costuming and music, and that means meticulous research.

And because there are only two continuing characters—Sam and Al—guest stars play unusually prominent parts and have to be integrated into the production at a breakneck pace. And, of course, there are the complex storylines and the technically demanding special effects.

A typical day on location often begins at eight in the morning and runs for twelve, fourteen or more hours. What follows is the behind-the-scenes view of one visitor with full access.

The Location

"It's a strange business that goes out and sets up a factory at a new location every day," observes second assistant director Brian Faul, a bearded young man with a bemused, but competent air.

This day, "the factory" is setting up at a Los Angeles landmark, the long-closed Ambassador Hotel. It's a sprawling relic from Hollywood's Gilded Age that once was home to the Cocoanut Grove nightclub, where, in the fifties, you might come for an elegant evening of formal dining and dancing among the potted palms and the black-leather art-deco furnishings, perhaps, to hear Nat King Cole sing.

The Ambassador has a long history, but perhaps it's best known to the general public as the site of the Bobby Kennedy assassination in 1968.

This week, for the first time in years, the hotel is welcoming visitors—the approximately ninety-person cast and crew from *Quantum Leap*, who will, in the next few days, transform different parts of the hotel into a variety of sets, including a Fifties East Coast nightclub, a roadside diner, and a Las Vegas casino.

The Episode: "Stand Up"

It's April 30, 1959 and Sam leaps in in the middle of a comedy act that's playing a seedy nightclub with a tough, heckling audience. He's Parker of Parker & MacKay, and MacKay is an egomaniac with a short temper.

The act is saved by Frankie, a waitress with a beehive hairdo, natural comic timing and a crush on Mack. Her impromptu jokes warm up the unfriendly audience and Parker, MacKay, and Frankie go on to the Las Vegas big time.

Mack is played by comedian-actor Bob Saget (*Full House, America's Funniest Home Videos*), for whom the part was written.

9:00 A.M.

The crew has already been around for an hour, dividing into separate "companies" and work groups. One group is busily turning a coffee shop into a fifties roadside diner; another is turning the intimate Palm Bar into a smoky nightclub; a third is in the high-ceilinged Sunset Ballroom, setting up scaffolding in front of a two-story high "blue screen."

Yet another group is crowded into a narrow, dank basement hallway, which is doubling for the backstage dressing area of a seedy nightclub, circa 1959.

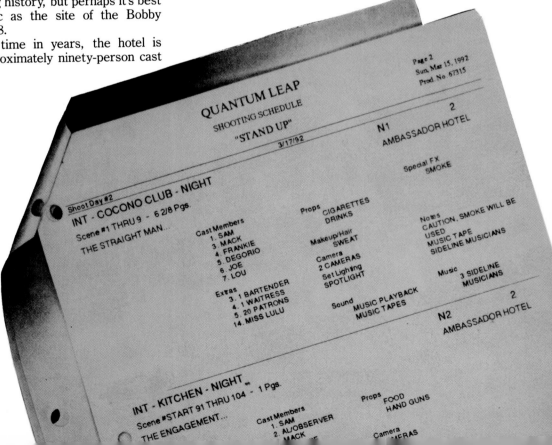

156

Lights are going up in the hallway, cables snake across the floor; a massive Panavision camera is wheeled into place, while a rack of video monitors and a soundboard are brought in and hooked up. A tiny bathroom doubles for the makeup area.

A technician is taping color-coded "marks" on the floor so that the actors will know where to stand. Another is measuring the distance from the camera's lens to various precise spots in the shot.

Hammers are pounding, crew members call out to each other, trading raucous jokes; everyone, it seems, is clutching a crackling walkie-talkie.

"Okay, copy that. Back to One, back to one...."

"If you'd give me an accurate update, I'd appreciate it."

"Looks like the First Team is coming in."

"Okay, ten minutes."

While the crew finishes setting up, the visitor wanders outdoors and finds the pastry and coffee cart. A tall, gawky, black-haired man with a youthful look lopes up. He's wearing a loud fifties checkered sport coat and a matching bow tie over brown slacks and shoes. In person, Bob Saget is as boyish and bright-eyed as he is on television.

"So, you're playing Jerry Lewis to Scott's Dean Martin?"

"I guess you could say that," Saget replies. "I'm basically basing it on comics that I've known over the years."

And why is he subjecting himself to this brutal pace during his time off from his own two shows?

"I'm friends with a lot of the people [who produce the show]."

"Aren't you tired?"

"Yeah, but I like the show. *Full House* wrapped [for the season]. And *Videos* has five more [episodes] to go. I was writing *Videos* from here last night," he adds, flashing his trademark crooked smile. "That's the kind of guy I am. An overachiever."

9:30 A.M.

The buzz of activity in the narrow hallway continues as a sandy-haired, bespectacled, young-looking man ambles in. He's co-executive producer Michael Zinberg, a television veteran directing this episode.

"Okay, let us rehearse, please," he says quietly, and immediately crew members begin shushing each other into silence.

On cue, the actors appear: Scott Bakula, in a baggy, fifties blue suit with a narrow red tie; Saget; actress Amy Yasbeck, who's playing the waitress Frankie, and Wil Albert, a silver-haired actor in a swirly red tuxedo, who's playing the angry nightclub owner.

One of the techies trips on a cable. "You should walk a mile in my pumps," Yasbeck quips as she totters by.

"I guess you're all wondering why we're here today," Zinberg calls out. "Let's get a rehearsal and we'll find out."

More buzzing, more shushing.

"Quiet, quiet, please," says one of the assistant directors.

"Okay, rehearsal! Quiet for rehearsal!"

Saget goes behind a door decorated with a star and his character's name. Bakula and Yasbeck hit their marks; the nightclub owner waits tensely just out of camera range, silently mouthing his lines.

"Okay... *rehearsal!*"

Although at least a dozen people are crowded around the actors, it's now silent in the narrow passageway.

"Ready, and..."

The camera's rolling.

"*Action!*"

Frankie and Mack have just had an argument; now, Frankie, near tears, faces the closed door of Mack's dressing room.

FRANKIE

He's the most selfish, self-centered egomaniac I've ever had the misfortune to meeting in my life!

Sam tries to console her.

SAM

Yeah, but how do you *really* feel about the guy?

FRANKIE

I'm crazy about him. You know Mack. He can be so sweet. When we first went out he used to hold my chair and help me with my coat. He would light my cigarette and I don't even smoke. Then you offered to give me a shot and he turned into... a futz!

The angry nightclub owner bursts into the scene.

OWNER

Where's that partner of yours?

SAM

Mack?

OWNER

What other idiot partner have you got? *(to Frankie)* I ain't counting you, 'cause you deserve better.

The dressing room door flies open and Mack comes out like a hurricane.

MACK

(a beat)

Better than what? You don't get any better than Parker and MacKay! And you're damn lucky to have us in this two-bit, run-down, cheap...

SAM

Uh... Mack. I don't think it's such a good idea...

MACK

...hole in the wall dive.

SAM

...to bite the...

OWNER

You're fired!

SAM

...hand that feeds you.

Sam shoots a look of disgust at a spot on the wall where Al will later be blue-screened in.

SAM

Thanks for the advance warning.

OWNER

You got all the warning you need.

MACK

You can't fire me!

OWNER

Watch me, I'll do it again!

SAM

Why don't we sit down and talk about this?

OWNER

You're fired! How was that?

Suddenly, Mack slugs the nightclub owner. As Sam and Frankie try to pull him away....

The four actors, locked-together in mock battle, move out of camera range, and....

"Okay," Zinberg says. "Is that a two-inch lens?" he asks the cameraman.

"Yes, sir."

"Let's try a three-inch," he suggests, going over to consult with the actors, telling Saget he wants him to come out of the dressingroom with even more intensity and offering Yasbeck another way to read her lines, with her emotional intensity peaking on a different word than in the first take.

"We ready to roll again?" he asks, turning to the cameraman.

"Loading camera one," he replies, as a kidney-shaped reel of film is attached to the top of the camera. "Ready now, sir."

"Okay, camera run-through."

Saget and Bakula are trading jokes. "Get back in your room, Bob," one of the technicians calls out.

Bakula shrugs, shadow boxes with the camera.

"Quiet! Could we have it quiet down the hall, please!"

More shushing; for a moment the hallway sounds like a wind tunnel.

"Okay, picture!"

Someone, somewhere, is whistling.

"Okay, very quiet now!"

Abruptly, the whistling stops.

"And...*rolling!*"

"Marker!"

A kid with a clapboard, on which is written *Scene 12-A, Take 2,* steps in front of the camera. Clap! And he steps back out of the shot.

"Action!"

The actors take it from the top. At the end of the shot, as they struggle out of the frame, someone calls out, "Hey, you guys are having fun together!"

A few of the crew members whistle and applaud.

"Quiet! Quiet!" someone yells out testily. "I hear music! Somebody's playing music!"

"Sounds like it's coming from downstairs," the sound man says, removing his headphones. A crew member is dispatched to silence the nearly inaudible sounds.

"Okay, let's do it again!"

Zinberg consults with Saget, who's distracted by an off-camera stagehand, who's standing in his line-of-sight. An assistant moves all the unnecessary crew members out of the way.

"Bob," Zinberg says after a moment, "everybody who's there now has to be there. The eyeline's clear."

Saget makes a joke about bringing in the coffee-cart man to do the scene, setting off another round of stagehand quips. Off to the side, Bakula begins singing in a high-pitched rock 'n' roll falsetto: *"Way down inside, woman, you need me..."* A couple of the crew take up the tune.

"Very quiet, please!"

Everyone moves to their marks.

Bakula is still singing. *"Way, way down inside...."*

"Rolling!"

Clap!

"Action!"

They go through the scene again.

"Okay, that's a cut," says Zinberg, when the actors go rolling out of frame. "Let's do it again."

"Action!"

Take four is stopped midway through when the sound man picks up construction noises from another part of the hotel.

Another crew member is sent to investigate. After a few moments, his voice crackles over a walkie-talkie. "It's a compressor going down here."

They do it again. And again. And again.

After each time, the director offers quiet suggestions to the three visiting actors, changing an inflection here, a position there. Bakula, though, seems to have his moves and his lines down cold.

Between takes a makeup woman touches up Yasbeck's lipstick, when the director calls out, "Okay, action!"

Bakula grins. "I'm not ready," he says gallantly, winking in the makeup woman's direction. She hurriedly finishes and dashes out of the shot.

"Here we go. Right from the top...."

After seven takes, it's a wrap. "Thank you," says the ever-polite, unflappable director.

The crew members start to break down the set; the actors head for another scene, in another part of the hotel.

11:00 A.M.

The Palm Bar, off the main lobby, is dark wood and red velvet, with gleaming bottles lined up behind the bar. There's a small stage at one end of the room.

Stagehands are hanging movie posters from the fifties on the walls—*Witness for the Prosecution, Come Back Little Sheba, A Streetcar Named Desire.*

Others are placing colored lights behind the potted palms. Two big cameras are wheeled in, as a troup of extras take their places at tables in the audience.

They're about to rehearse the opening scene, in which a dazed-looking Sam "leaps in" into the middle of the Parker and MacKay lounge act. Sam has to endure the taunts of a drunken heckler when he can't tell his jokes. In the scene Frankie saves him by coming on stage and improvising a funny story. The scene opens like this:

FADE IN
CLOSE ON SAM

A blinding light fills the screen and then conforms into a discombobulated Sam. He blinks and is hit with a sharp punch to the arm, spilling the drink he's holding. He tries to get his balance looking around.

MACK'S VOICE

Sooo... what did the cop say?

INTERIOR—SMALL NIGHT CLUB STAGE—TWO SHOT—FEATURING SAM.

He stands next to a tall man with mussed hair. His name is Mack MacKay. He wears a wild print jacket and a silly expression. From his expression, Mack is obviously perturbed by Sam's behavior.

SAM

I... I'm sorry, what did you say?

MACK

I said, sooo... what did the cop say?

SAM

Cop?

HECKLER'S VOICE

He probably said you should get yourself a day job.

MACK

What did you do? Escape from a home for the verbally challenged or just the hopelessly stupid?

There's an uncomfortable titter from the small audience. Sam turns and looks into the spotlight, squinting at the crowd.

The room is about half-full and it's a pretty tough crowd. Sam's eyes widen as he realizes where he is.

SAM

I... uh... he... was... uh...

MACK

(prompting)
He was hauling you in and...

SAM

The cop, oh... yes, I was...

MACK

Naked.

SAM

Naked!

MACK

Hiding in the bushes...

SAM

In the bushes?

MACK

(prompting)
Holding the sheep and you said...

SAM

Oh boy.

FADE OUT

While the crew works, Bakula and Saget—both in shirtsleeves, holding scripts—take their places on the small stage. Director Zinberg eases himself into a lounge chair in the center of the "audience."

"Okay, here we go, ladies and gentlemen," a voice calls out from the back of the room. But there's a snag: actress Amy Yasbeck has lost her shoes.

"Where'd you leave them, Amy? We'll send somebody for them, dear."

"That's okay," you actress sniffs in mock-teary voice. "I'll be okay without them. No, really, it's okay."

The rehearsal begins.

"Quiet! We are rehearsing!"

"Zzzzzzzzz!" goes the director. "And... Leap in!"

"*Sooo... what did the cop say?*"

The actors run through the lines, over and over again, the director gently cutting in to offer suggestions, change lines and sharpen the timing and the focus of the scene.

"I'm going to flip a line here," he says, while the script supervisor makes the change he calls for in her thick notebook. "You tried it with the mike last time," he says after Saget has put down the heckler, "Try it without the mike now."

After about an hour, they break.

While the crew finishes dressing the set, the actors head for their respective trailers to learn their lines. And Zinberg and a visitor wander out to the coffee cart for a talk.

"I was with the show as a director the first season," Zinberg recalls, "and as a producer starting midway in the second season."

"Got a favorite episode that you directed?"

"It would have to be Vietnam."

"Tell me why? Is it close to your experience?"

"First of all, it was written by Don. It was a war that touched my generation and myself deeply. It was about Scott saving his brother's life.

"It was a magnificent shoot," he adds, "a situation where the entire cast and crew pitched in and did some extraordinary things in nine days—skiing behind a helicopter, war scenes; incredibly emotional moments—all out in a makeshift jungle. And it got to the screen."

Zinberg pauses a moment. "And I won the Directors Guild award for it," he adds, almost shyly.

"What's the most challenging part of all this? It looks like chaos on the surface."

"The most challenging part is that we start fresh every episode," he says. "In eight or nine days, we create a little movie every single time."

"And what is it that you bring to the party?"

"Well, with Scott and Dean there's not much. Dean, he's the young old pro.... He's incredibly technically knowledgeable. About the only thing you need to do with Scott is to keep him on track with what Sam knows and doesn't know, because we shoot out of sequence."

"Is set construction and costuming a huge expense for this show?"

"Enormously expensive, enormously expensive."

"How much?"

"Set construction's about sixty thousand dollars an episode, and wardrobes can be twenty-five to thirty thousand or as much as sixty thousand for an episode."

"And how much does a typical episode cost?"

"Depending on the episode, it runs between a million four-fifty and a million five an episode."

If Zinberg sounds knowledgeable, it's because he's a young old pro himself, having directed episodes of *L.A. Law* and *Midnight Caller* and "going all the way back" to *Lou Grant, Taxi, Family Ties, Cheers,* and *The Bob Newhart Show.*

If he sounds faintly professorial, it's because in his spare time he also teaches at his alma mater, the University of Texas in Austin.

"I'm involved with the College of Communications down there," Zinberg says. "I teach a Master class in directing, a Master class in writing and I give basic introductory seminars to what the business is like and how things work in television primetime."

And what does he tell his writing students about *Quantum Leap?*

"When we lay out a story, the most important thing to Don [Bellisario] is the heart of the story—you know, what's at stake for Scott and why do we want to tell this story."

And what advice has he been whispering to his guest-star actress all day?

"She's really good, and she's working really nice in this part," Zinberg says. "I wanted her to do some different things, to try one [take] a little angrier, to try one a little more comedic, to try one being a little less frustrated. I was just looking for shades, so that when I go into the cutting room and edit the show together, I've got some choices."

A crew member breaks into the conversation. "Is there a kosher doctor in the house?" he cries out in a nasal accent. "Is there a kosher doctor?"

The director shrugs. "I guess they're ready for me again."

Back inside the Palm Bar, a smoke machine is billowing, the extras and the actors are all in costume and, from the back of the darkened room, a voice calls out, "Anyone wearing beepers or late-model watches, please take them off."

The shooting resumes.

1:00 P.M.

Deborah Pratt is a woman of many hats—writer, actress, producer...admiral.

Today, as she strides cowboy-booted past the trailer-and-truck encampment in an Ambassador parking lot, the co-executive producer and author of the episode currently being shot, also has on a white baseball cap, with a long white bill decorated with enough military-style gold leaf to make her an admiral at least.

"Hiya, chief," grunts one of the teamsters sitting around a battered card table in the parking lot, when she stops momentarily to kibitz at the drivers' all-day poker game.

She greets all the men around the table by name, before joining a visitor to the set. Pratt is wearing a fashionably

oversized black coat over a white sweater and tight black jeans tucked into her white-and-gold boots.

In addition to writing "fourteen or fifteen" of the show's scripts, she starred as Troian in "Portrait of Troian," a Halloween episode.

She's not in front of cameras very often anymore, she says, adding with a musical laugh, "They keep me pretty busy [here]."

Of the shows she's written, her own favorite is "Shock Theatre," the episode in which Sam leaps into a mental institution and is given shock therapy that turns his previous leap-incarnations into multiple personalities. "It was a real tour de force for Scott," she says, "and it was real fun to write, because for me it really integrated a lot of the shows."

"And I liked him being pregnant and a woman," she adds, "because I've been pregnant twice, so it was neat to watch Scott in labor for two days."

Considering her vast *Quantum Leap* writing experience, it seems odd that this episode has no "kiss with history." She laughs, allowing that writer Pratt *did* write it in, but that co-executive producer Pratt agreed to take it out.

"Originally, they're driving across country and Mack [guest star Bob Saget] looks out the window and goes, 'What the hell is that?' And you look out and you see that, in 1959, it's a Volkswagen bug. And Sam goes, 'It's called a Beetle.' [Mack] says, "It looks like a Beetle." [And Sam] says, 'It's an import car from Germany. We start letting those cars in, who knows what's going to happen to the auto industry.'"

Pratt originally wrote the part of Mack with Bob Saget in mind. "He's been a fan of the show for a long time. I lucked-out and got to see his stand-up act, and I saw a lot of that very fast, reality-based, stream-of-consciousness humor, so I tried to incorporate that, and created a character that was very different than he played in *Full House,* which is always the nice guy.

"I wanted him to be challenged," she continues, "so I gave him some romance and...a real angry person to play."

In general, though, the toughest shows to write are the ones Pratt calls the "bottle shows that take place in one place." In one bottle show Sam is in prison and in another he is on the Queen Mary. "You literally have to write a little play, so it's really a challenge as a writer to write an entire act in one room," says Pratt, clearly a woman who likes challenges.

Of her many hats which is her favorite? "There is a high in performing that you don't get any other place," she replies. "There's a creativity in writing that is limitless. And as a producer it's the power of saying, 'No I want the dress to be green, or the room to be this, or let's cut it this way, or I want forties music in here,' and it's putting it all together."

She notices a crew member, clipboard in hand, waiting nearby. She's needed to make a decision. But before she goes, the visitor wants to know if a woman-in-charge producer has trouble getting respect from a tough, good ol' boy Hollywood crew. "Sure," she says lightly, but there's a touch of weariness to her voice. "Usually I'm nice the first couple of times.

"Once, there was something that I requested that wasn't done and they were waiting for someone else to tell them what to do, and I said, 'This is the way that I want it, this is my show; unless you have a problem, or know somebody that wants different.' And they said [they didn't] and then they went on and did exactly what they wanted to do, and I came back down and said, 'Now we're going to shoot it again. We're going to change it and we're going to do it the way I requested it the first time.'" Then she smiles sweetly and leaves.

2:00 P.M.

Harold Frizzell doesn't look anything like Scott Bakula. But the powerfully built, white-haired show-business veteran, who has a rugged cowboy look and a laid-back demeanor, is exactly the actor's height, and that's why Frizzell has been "standing in" for Bakula for four seasons.

In a business that has a lot of hurry-up-and-wait, Frizzell's job comes with more hanging out time than most, so he's more than willing to explain his duties and spin tales of a Hollywood era now past.

"I stand in to block scenes, do the lighting and stuff," he says with a laconic drawl. "I've had lights dropped on my head. I had a set of barndoors...that fell and hit me on the head. Put fourteen stitches in it.

"Other than that, why, you have to be careful 'bout when they set the lights and when they're lightin' 'em, because they can really damage your eyes, especially with the new lights that they have.... You learn to look, but not look into the lights."

Frizzel has also been in front of the *Quantum Leap* cameras. "When he did the pregnant lady, I was the orderly in it. I was the one that was shovin' him down the hall into the operatin' room. I've done a lot of background stuff. Y'know: crossin', drivin' taxis, drivin' a car in the shot and stuff."

He's also stood-in on *The FBI, Alias Smith and Jones,* and *Emergency,* where Frizzell was the stunt double for one of the leads. "The toughest stunt I ever did was comin' outa the top of the King Dome in Seattle, rappeling out of the top of it and into a cage," he recalls. "It was three hundred eighty-six feet. I had to come down sixty feet, then swing over into a cage, rescue a guy, then rappel the rest of the way down. That was *Emergency.* We did a lot of fire gags on that show. I was constantly bein' blowed-up and blowed-out."

He is called back to the set in mid-reminiscence about working with John Wayne, and the next time the visitor sees him he's standing patiently in the Palm Bar set, carefully *not* looking directly into the blinding spotlight that's focused on his face.

3:00 P.M.

Lunch break. The cast and crew troop across the wide expanse of lawn outside the hotel and form a line at the catering truck.

The food's hot and there's plenty to choose from—roast turkey and stuffing, mashed potatoes and gravy, pork chops, sauerkraut and cabbage, mixed vegetables, cooked spinach and green salads, cakes, pies, ice cream, soft drinks, tea, and coffee.

"You're lucky, dear," says the show's chief of security, Martha Harris, a curly-haired blond with a Missouri twang, who moonlights as country-western singer, "it's the good caterer today."

Three long trestle tables, each covered by a blue-and-white checkered cloth and seating about thirty, are set up on the lawn.

As the tables fill up with hungry people, Scott Bakula and a couple of crew members—wearing gym clothes, sweat shirts and tennis shoes, and carrying hockey sticks and rollerblades—stride purposefully past.

"Let the games begin," someone mutters between bites.

4:30 P.M.

Inside the Palm Bar, they're still going at it. In the lobby a group of extras, all in fifties costumes, are choosing period eyeglasses from a prop man's case.

When an assistant director walks by, one of the extras asks how long it will be before they wrap for the day.

The A.D. scratches his chin. "Oh, we'll be done by seven-thirty, eight," he says innocently.

A paunchy technician passing by snorts derisively. "Don't B. S. 'em. No way we get out of here before ten-thirty tonight."

The extra, on his first *Leap* day, looks astounded.

8:30 P.M.

On the diner set period signs are going up: Top Sirloin Steak Dinner—30 cents.

In the massive basement kitchen yet another scene is being rehearsed.

In the Sunset Banquet Room Dean Stockwell—resplendent in an apricot-colored suit and a matching shirt and tie—is standing in front of the huge blue screen, calmly puffing on a cigar, while technicians pore over video monitors, matching his image to the morning's shots.

That crew member was right, the visitor realizes as he trudges wearily out into the cool L.A. night. Behind him, inside the vast landmark hotel, now looming portentously in the dark, the cast and crew work on.

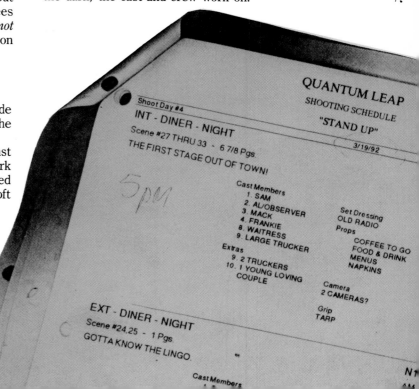

DEAN AND SCOTT, DON AND DEBORAH: The Official Bios

"Official" network and studio biographies are curious documents, often with a conveniently selective recall of the salient facts, as any reporter on the show business beat will tell you.

If, for example, a movie star is involved in a spectacular screen failure, that picture often fails to make its way onto the "official" list of the star's credits. And of course the "official" age of many stars remains perennially unchanged.

The four official bios that follow, however, tell it fairly straight. There's one exception, and it can simply be written off to the sloppiness of the anonymous public relations writer rather than anything more sinister:

The "official" bio says that Dean Stockwell made his precocious stage debut at the age of six, after his *father* took him to an audition. You know from this book that it was his *mother* who took him down to that theater, albeit at his father's suggestion.

DEAN STOCKWELL: The Official Bio

Dean Stockwell, who earned an Academy Award nomination for his role in the hit film *Married to the Mob,* and both popular and critical plaudits for his starring role in *Tucker,* is enjoying what many call the major comeback of the decade.

He currently stars in Universal's award-winning NBC series, *Quantum Leap,* portraying the wisecracking scientist/holographic observer, Albert, and has received a Golden Globe as Best Supporting Actor.

What spurred him, after a long and successful career in motion pictures, to make the leap to television? "As a mountain climber would say, because it's there. I've never done a series, and I welcome the experience. The character particularly attracted me because he's zany, colorful and comedic. Before *Married to the Mob* came along, I'd never done comedy, and now people realize I'm good at it."

Stockwell today finds himself one of the busiest actors in Hollywood with several upcoming feature films, including *Sandino* with Kris Kristofferson and Robert Altman's *The Player.*

He was seen in the critically acclaimed ABC-TV miniseries *Son of the Morning Star,* and his appearance in David Lynch's *Blue Velvet* made many aware of the range and depth of this consummate actor.

In short, after having been thrust into an often unhappy career as a child actor, and after twice dropping out of show business, Stockwell finds himself a happy man who's in demand.

As a child, he starred in such classics as *Anchors Aweigh,* the celebrated *The Boy With Green Hair* and *Kim;* as a young man, in films such as *Compulsion,* for which he won a Golden Globe and the prestigious Cannes Film Festival Award for Best Actor.

His pivotal role in *Long Day's Journey Into Night* stands side-by-side with his memorable performances in *Paris, Texas, To Live and Die in L.A., Gardens of Stone, Beverly Hills Cop II, Limit Up* and *Palais Royale.*

Stockwell was six years old when his father Harry, a musical comedy performer (and the voice of Prince Charming in the Disney film *Snow White*) took him to a New York audition. Before he really knew what was happening, he was cast as the lead on stage in *Innocent Voyage.* A savvy talent scout spotted him, and he was quickly whisked off to Hollywood.

No one asked him if he wanted to be an actor. "I quit the business when I was sixteen," he says. "I cut my hair off, changed my name and disappeared into the countryside. For five years, I did odd jobs and then, when I ran out of things to do, I went back into the business to try again."

It wasn't long before he went on to star in *Compulsion,* a trailblazing film that enjoyed a phenomenal success, and in 1962's memorable *Long Day's Journey Into Night,* with Katharine Hepburn, Ralph Richardson, and Jason Robards. Then it came time to escape again. "In the sixties, when we had hippies and Haight-Ashbury, I dropped out of my career and went with all that.

"I found that very fulfilling because I didn't have much of a childhood first time around," he says.

His subsequent return to the business wasn't quite as easy. There were occasional roles on television and in films, but it wasn't until some ten years ago when he met his wife, Joy, and started a family—they have a son, Austin, and a daughter, Sophia—and moved to New Mexico, and he suddenly found himself in demand again.

Dean currently lives in Los Angeles where, along with his wife, he devotes much of his time to attempting to educate the public about environmental issues, with particular emphasis on the perils inherent in the ongoing depletion of the ozone layer.

SCOTT BAKULA: The Official Bio

In the innovative one-hour series Bakula stars as Sam Beckett, a scientist whose experiment with time travel goes awry and leaves him trapped between the fifties and the nineties, while he attempts to find his way back to the present day.

The *New York Times* says, "Scott Bakula has the most demanding and rewarding job on weekly television. Mr. Bakula jumps from one character to another with thoroughly impressive and charming aplomb... this actor seems to revel in versatility."

For his performance, Bakula received a 1992 Golden Globe Award for Best Performance by an Actor in a Television Series Drama. In addition to receiving two Emmy nominations and two Golden Globe nominations for his role in *Quantum Leap,* Bakula was honored with the Viewers For Quality Television Award for Best Actor in a Drama for two consecutive years.

While on hiatus from the series, Bakula keeps up his frenetic pace by working on both a feature film and a movie for television. Recently, he made his starring feature-film debut in the Paramount comedy, *Necessary Roughness,* portraying a thirty-four-year-old freshman quarterback for a group of outlandish and unconventional college athletes.

The *Los Angeles Times* stated in their review of the film, "Scott Bakula scores... Bakula has a laid-back quality that makes him a welcome, easy-to-take presence on the big screen." Bakula also stars in the NBC movie-of-the-week *An Eye for an Eye,* playing an undercover New York City cop who finds himself ostracized from the force when he takes a public stand against the death penalty.

Before making his mark on television, however, Scott was already a well-known theater actor. He won a 1988 Tony nomination for his starring role in the Broadway musical *Romance/Romance.*

Bakula made his feature film debut in 1990 opposite Kirstie Alley in *Sibling Rivalry,* directed by Carl Reiner.

Born in St. Louis, Bakula had originally planned to follow in his father's footsteps as a lawyer, before deciding on an acting career. Moving to New York in 1976 he made his Broadway debut as Joe DiMaggio in *Marilyn: An American Fable.* He went on to appear in the critically acclaimed Off Broadway production of *3 Guys Naked From the Waist Down,* which he later performed at the Pasadena Playhouse. Before his return to Broadway in *Romance,* Bakula appeared in both the Los Angeles and Boston productions of *Nite Club Confidential.*

An accomplished singer, sometime dancer, pianist and composer, Bakula's favorite role in life is undoubtedly husband and father. Currently he resides in Los Angeles with his wife and children.

Ask Bakula if he has any second thoughts about choosing to become an actor instead of a lawyer and you'll find the answer on a stage, screen or television near you.

DONALD PAUL BELLISARIO: The Official Bio

Donald Paul Bellisario is the creator and executive producer of *Quantum Leap* and *Tequila and Bonetti*, as well as the creator of such other highly successful television series as *Magnum, P.I.*

In 1965 Don became a copywriter for a small advertising agency in Lancaster, Pennsylvania, and three years later he moved to Dallas to become creative director of the nationally known Bloom Agency. By 1976, after eight years at Bloom, Bellisario was senior vice president, creative director, and a member of the board of directors.

Moving to Hollywood, Bellisario was a producer on *Baa Baa Black Sheep* for a year, and then supervising producer on *Battlestar Gallactica* before becoming involved in development. He created *Magnum, P.I.*, the series that made Tom Selleck an international star, as well as *Tales of the Gold Monkey* and *Airwolf*, serving as executive producer on all three.

In 1987 Bellisario's first feature *Last Rites,* which he wrote, produced and directed, starred Tom Berenger as a priest who uses his church to shelter a young woman from the Mafia. By that time, he had begun development on *Quantum Leap,* a show that lets him explore his interest in recent history, as well as a variety of television formats: comedy, social commentary, action adventure.

Don was born in Cokeburg, Pennsylvania. Apart from flying helicopters, Bellisario is an avid golfer (handicap: 9).

DEBORAH PRATT: The Official Bio

Deborah Pratt, writer and co-executive producer of *Quantum Leap,* is an all-around show-business professional.

Comfortable in the role of writer and executive, she is also an actress, dancer, comedienne, singer, and songwriter.

Born in Chicago to an investment banker father and a teacher/psychologist mother, she comes from a family of high achievers: of her three sisters, one is a microsurgeon, another a city planner in Washington and a third was in pre-veterinary medicine before coming to Los Angeles to enter theatrical production.

Pratt has loved show business since she was a child. Her parents wanted her to have professional training, and she attended Webster College, where she earned a B.A. in psychology while taking theater courses.

After graduation, she took a teaching job in Chicago's inner city. "It shocked me into reality," Pratt recalls. "I wanted to find a way of affecting people emotionally and make them feel good about being who they are."

It was this drive that led her to pursue a career in show business, writing and performing for children. She appeared on stage in *Don't Bother Me, I Can't Cope,* was one of Dean Martin's "Golddiggers" on television in Hollywood and began appearing on the major variety shows of the early nineteen-seventies.

Although she sang and wrote songs for two successful albums, Deborah began to study drama and comedy with Harvey Lembeck, who has also taught John Ritter and Robin Williams.

As she began to perform more on television, she found the number and quality of roles available to African-Americans unfulfilling, and started writing more herself. At Columbia Television she developed what would have been the first integrated soap opera, a decade before the recent *Generations.* "I acted to keep writing and wrote to keep acting," Pratt says of her entwined careers.

As a producer on *Quantum Leap,* Pratt feels that she can accomplish what she decided to do in that inner-city school twenty years ago: "I can do stories that affect people, and remind them that they can make a difference."

Her contribution to *Quantum* has taken the show into such controversial topics as sexual harassment and racial prejudice. Areas that, according to Brandon Tartikoff at NBC, were key in keeping *Quantum* on the air their first few years.